THE SECOND CREATION

Genetic Engineering of Man

THE SECOND CREATION
Genetic Engineering of Man

William C. Klingensmith III, MD

Wick Publishing, Inc., Englewood, Colorado

William C. Klingensmith III, MD
Cherry Hills Village, Colorado
United States

ISBN: 0692891811
ISBN 9780692891810 (Print)
ISBN 978-0-692-89180-3 (eBook)

To all those who came before, who carried the genome of homo sapiens
through the ages and into the twenty-first century.
And who suffered from innumerable genetic abnormalities and mutations
for which there was no prevention and no cure.

And to all those who in the twenty-first century will be entrusted
with the transition to genetically engineered man.
May they possess and demonstrate exceptional knowledge and wisdom,
and courage and compassion.
In hopes that homo engineerium will represent and preserve
the best of humankind,
And that these genes will be distributed equitably throughout the species.

Foreword

Normally, a foreword is written by someone other than the author. In this case, the *Foreword* was written by the author thirty years after the book was first created. I originally completed this book in 1987, but it wasn't published until now, 2017. This foreword explains and bridges the gap.

I have been fascinated by genetics for as long as I can remember. The first time I ever borrowed a book from a teacher was in tenth grade. My biology teacher had a thick book on human genetics on her desk. I borrowed it, took it home, and read it from cover to cover. At that time human genetics consisted only of clinical observations and a rudimentary knowledge of genes, but essentially no molecular biology.

In college I majored in zoology and then went to medical school. I thought about specializing in clinical genetics, but the field was still limited to simple diagnosis and no therapy. I ended up specializing in radiology and subspecializing in nuclear medicine.

Then in 1978 in England, Patrick Steptoe, an obstetrician and gynecologist, and Robert Edwards, an embryologist, produced the first test-tube baby, Louise Joy Brown. This event established in vitro fertilization as a viable alternative for infertile couples. For this work Edwards was awarded the 2010 Nobel Prize in Physiology or Medicine. (Steptoe was no longer living and, therefore, ineligible to share the award.)

In 1983 Howard and Georgeanna Jones, both gynecologists, were responsible for the first test-tube baby in the United States. As the Joneses were my parents-in-law, I had a front-row seat to subsequent controversies and progress in assisted reproductive technology and reproductive medicine.

Because of my interest in human genetics, my exposure to the development of in vitro fertilization, and, to no small extent, my fascination with the newly introduced, easy-to-use, Macintosh personal computer, I embarked on writing a novel titled, *The Second Creation: Genetic Engineering of Man*. I finished the book in 1987, but it never found a publisher, perhaps the story was ahead of its time.

Getting a scientific manuscript published, which is what I normally do, is, in comparison, relatively easy. You submit the manuscript to an appropriate scientific journal, and the editor assigns it to two knowledgeable reviewers. They review the manuscript and recommend for or against publication. The editor then returns the anonymous reviews to the author(s) with the publication decision. If the first journal decides not to publish the paper, you incorporate any good suggestions from the reviewers and resubmit the paper to the next journal, usually a less selective one. You repeat the process until the paper is accepted.

But in the case of a novel, traditional print publishers receive so many amateur attempts by unpublished authors hoping to write the next great American novel that the manuscript may not even get a reading. In 1987 the process was first to submit a three-page synopsis of the novel. If the publisher liked the synopsis, they asked for three sample chapters. If they liked the three sample chapters, they asked for the entire manuscript. I got to the last stage once before my manuscript was rejected.

Now there is another viable alternative. Computers and the Internet have spawned e-books, which are inexpensive to produce and distribute. In 2007, Amazon created Kindle Direct Publishing which allows anyone to upload, publish and sell his/her own e-book. In 2016, Amazon released 4 million e-titles and 40 percent of them were self-published. Surprisingly, that year the self-published e-books accounted for 25 percent of Amazon's $2.3 billion in e-book revenue including several best sellers (1). Print publishing has also been positively affected by computers and the Internet.

It is interesting to note the scientific advances that have occurred and have not occurred since *The Second Creation: Genetic Engineering of Man* was written thirty years ago. In 1987 the human genome had not yet been sequenced and the number of genes was estimated at approximately one hundred thousand. When the Human Genome Project was completed in 2003 and the markers for genes were counted only about twenty-seven thousand genes were found (2). Most of the DNA did not code for proteins and was called "junk DNA." Subsequently, it was found that much of the junk DNA plays a regulatory role in gene function.

When this book was written, the section at the end of the book, titled *Milestones in the Genetic Engineering of Man*, listed fifteen milestones beginning with the origin of life on earth 3.7 billion years ago. More recent evidence suggests that primitive life originated much earlier, around 4.4 billion years ago (3). Of the fifteen milestones the first thirteen had already been achieved and were followed by two anticipated, but yet to be achieved, milestones. The two remaining milestones were: "The first successful use of genetic engineering in a human zygote is reported." and "A national program of genetic enhancement in man is begun." In 2015, scientists in China used a new, powerful gene-editing technique, CRISPR/Cas9, in nonviable human zygotes to edit and repair the hemoglobin gene responsible for thalassemia with limited success, but sufficient enough to qualify for the fourteenth milestone (4).

Currently, there is no known national program of genetic enhancement in the world so the fifteenth milestone remains unfulfilled.

In the past thirty years there have been numerous improvements in the biotechnology needed to edit a human genome, but the most remarkable one is CRISPR/Cas9 (5). Previously, using older techniques it would take a PhD graduate student in molecular biology his entire four to six years of training to create a new animal model with an altered gene. Now anyone with some instruction can accomplish the same feat in just a few days with readily available equipment and supplies. Another area of significant progress is bioengineering artificial genes and chromosomes although to date, this has been done only in simple biologic entities like bacteria and yeast (6,7). Because of these advances there has been broad recognition in the scientific community that the ability to genetically engineer man may be realized sooner than many had previously thought, and certainly sooner than the general public thinks possible.

It is hard to imagine a milestone that will be more important in the history of man than the realization of the genetic engineering of man (GEM). This will allow man to determine his own evolution. And, in turn, the path GEM takes will affect everything that man does and that man impacts, including the well-being of our shared planet.

The federal government will almost certainly regulate GEM so there is a need to educate the general public about the nature of GEM (8). One approach is to create one or more serious academic journals that would publish articles on an array of subjects related to GEM that would be of interest to a broad range of educated, intellectually curious members of the public. Another approach is a book like this one that covers the same topics in the format of a novel. Below is a partial list of the areas that will be affected by GEM, along with brief comments and predictions of the effect

GEM will have. In general, the associated comments and predictions are relatively optimistic and can be thought of as "GEM done right." However (spoiler alert), it is fully realized that many things could go wrong.

❖   ❖   ❖

Bioethics and GEM: In the past most bioethicists held the position that it would be unethical and possibly immoral to genetically engineer humans. However, as the technology has improved to the point that genetic engineering has become simpler, safer, and more accurate some bioethicists have come to the view that eventually it might be unethical *not* to perform genetic engineering, at least to correct genes that produce significant genetic disease.

Effect of GEM on health: Over the last few hundred years medicine has gone from providing almost no diagnostic capability and no treatment of significance to providing a great deal of worthwhile care. Correspondingly, the cost of medical care has increased dramatically because of high demand, and the expense of advanced pharmaceuticals and medical machines. While better and better health is certainly desirable, annual cost increases that significantly exceed inflation are unsustainable.

GEM may result in large cost savings in healthcare. It should be relatively straight forward to essentially eliminate diseases that are caused by a single dominant or recessive gene. In addition, as knowledge accumulates with respect to diseases that are caused by combinations of multiple genes, great progress in eliminating these diseases should also be possible. It would be useful for a team of clinical geneticists and health economists to estimate the potential cost savings based on the current understanding of genetic disease.

Effect of GEM on income inequality: In the post GEM era everyone will be talented and above average by current standards. This might result in a more cohesive society with greater empathy among citizens, and increased support for income policies that limit income inequality. A team of economists, sociologists, psychologists, and political scientists could analyze this issue.

Effect of GEM on marriage success: Presently, approximately 40 percent of marriages in the United States end in divorce. Over time analysis of marriage success compared to the genomes of marriage partners should allow society and counselors to predict which relationships are likely to lead to successful long-term marriages. In addition, the detrimental effect of divorce on children could be greatly reduced. A significant reduction in the divorce rate and consequent reduction in suboptimal child rearing would likely result in large cost savings.

Effect of GEM on the availability of workers for menial jobs: Assuming that society does not decide to intentionally genetically engineer individuals for the purpose of performing menial tasks there would be a shortage of workers for low skilled jobs. One way to solve this problem is to require that all people in their twenties spend two years performing menial jobs, somewhat like a military draft or peace corps. And over time, as robots become more and more capable, they could perform many of these menial jobs.

The effect of GEM on time spent in formal education: Currently, some exceptionally bright students enter college in their early teens and thrive. Clearly, there is potential to condense the traditional education pathway and save significant money and, at the same time, increase the length of an individual's productive lifetime. However, there may be social and developmental disadvantages for the child, family, and society. A team of educators, sociologists and psychologists could evaluate this issue.

Effect of GEM on educational institutions: In the post-GEM era essentially everyone will attend college and obtain the terminal degree in his or her field. And it is likely that research universities will supplant liberal art colleges. New knowledge is predominantly produced in research universities and a greater percentage of the population will be research scientists. With an increasing number of students whose talents lead them to want to be academic scientists the increased demand for research universities could be met by transforming liberal arts colleges into first-class research universities. The traditional liberal arts subjects would still be taught within research universities as they are now providing an excellent education for developing artists, musicians, writers, diplomats and other essential non-scientists.

Effect of GEM on politics:

Thomas Jefferson said,

> An enlightened citizenry is indispensable for the proper functioning of a republic. Self-government is not possible unless the citizens are educated sufficiently to enable them to exercise oversight. It is therefore imperative that the nation sees to it that a suitable education be provided for all its citizens.

He also said,

> I know no safe depository of the ultimate powers of the society but the people themselves; and if we think them not enlightened enough to exercise their control with a wholesome discretion, the remedy is not to take it from them, but to inform their discretion by education. This is the true corrective of abuses of constitutional power.

In the age of GEM, intelligent educated citizens will presumably be less likely fooled or manipulated by politicians seeking excessive power or unwise goals. It is also true that democratic countries are less likely to start wars than countries led by dictators. As humans become more uniformly intelligent the question of whether democracy will spread and dictators will fade will be of great interest. And in the same context, the question of whether dictators will try to use GEM to create a superior military will be of great concern.

Effect of GEM on the distribution of occupations: After "GEM done right" one can imagine a large shift in the distribution of occupations. The need for physicians and other healthcare workers outside of reproductive medicine and clinical genetics could decrease significantly. Likewise, with much greater income and talent equality, and the identification and elimination of genes that predispose to criminal behavior, the need for law enforcement personnel might also decrease with consequent cost savings. At the same time, more individuals with greater talents than in the pre-GEM era could be employed in research and development, which would drive a virtuous cycle of development of better technology (including more capable robots) that would free an ever-greater proportion of the population for research and development.

Effect of GEM on end-of-life issues: As molecular biology advances the possibility of significantly extending the life span of humans becomes increasingly achievable. Whether this should be pursued is a philosophical question, at least until one becomes elderly. However, eliminating disease and old-age frailty so a person is healthy until he or she dies peacefully in his or her sleep is widely supported, as envisioned in the poem, "The Wonderful One-Hoss Shay" by Oliver Wendell Holmes Sr.

Effect of GEM on enabling humans to keep pace with advances in culture: When fire was tamed by homo erectus about a million years ago, and the wheel was invented by homo sapiens around 3,500 BC, presumably everyone understood what had been done and how. Now with formalized education, a large number of dedicated researchers, and worldwide dissemination of knowledge there are new discoveries in theoretical mathematics and the physics of quantum mechanics that can only be understood by a relatively few, and these advances are occurring at a faster and faster pace. Thus, culture (including education) is evolving faster than the natural evolution of man. However, with GEM it is theoretically possible to engineer ever-smarter humans who can keep up with these abstract and complex intellectual achievements.

Selecting our children in the era of GEM: Currently, we "select" our children's genomes in a very crude way. Half of our children's genes come from each parent, but that half is determined by chance. We have some rough control over the selection of our spouse's genes based on our spouse's phenotype, but the success of this process is limited and it is very much an inexact science. Once GEM is fully implemented with a robust database of genomes and resultant phenotypes, we will have the option of unprecedented control over the physical and mental characteristics of our children. Maximum control in this process should be given to parents. However, the state will have to ensure that there is an appropriate distribution of talents and skills, and that problematic traits are not selected intentionally.

It might be decided that families to some extent specialize in certain talents so that if at least one parent is a gifted and satisfied musician then at least one of their children should be genetically engineered to be a great musician. On the other hand, requests by parents that are not in the interest of the child or society would be denied. In an actual case, a couple, who both had congenital deafness secondary to an autosomal dominant gene, wanted to use in vitro fertilization and preimplantation genetic diagnosis and selection to ensure that their child also had congenital deafness. The prospective parents used sign language and wanted to perpetuate this aspect of their family tradition. The hospital ethics committee denied their request (9). Other possibilities will be more problematic and will result in endless political debate. As an example, the issue of cloning or near cloning will be a contentious issue. The laws and regulations will undoubtedly vary among countries.

<u>Need for large scientific studies correlating genotypes with phenotypes</u>: It is impossible to do GEM optimally without a full understanding of the effects of a very large number of gene combinations on the resulting phenotypes over the lifetimes of a large number of individuals. This is a monumental task. Although a few small studies have been done and several larger ones are ongoing, a comprehensive cohort of individuals needs to be studied from conception to death. This will require nearly a hundred years, and GEM is likely to have started to a significant extent before then. The cost of such a study will be large, but the resulting knowledge will pay dividends indefinitely. A complementary approach is to initiate a project to acquire tissue for genomic sequencing from deceased individuals who are exceptionally talented, or possibly notorious. This might entail exhuming bodies of famous people.

The issues briefly discussed above are just a few of the important questions that deserve serious study and debate.

The novel that follows is intended to contribute to the process of public education and discussion of the various decisions, some easy and some very difficult, that will need to be made both before and after the biotechnology that enables safe and accurate genetic engineering of man becomes a reality. The novel is unchanged from thirty years ago except for updating a few scientific and geopolitical facts.

References

1. Alsever J: The Kindle effect. *Fortune* (January 2017): 32-33.
2. Alberts B, et al: *Molecular Biology of the Cell*, 5th edition, Garland Science, New York, 2008, 206.
3. Dodd MS, *et al.* Evidence for early life in Earth's oldest hydrothermal vent precipitates. *Nature,* 543: 60–64, 2017.
4. Cyranoski D, Reardon S: News. *Nature,* 22 April, 2015.
5. Travis J: 2015 Breakthrough of the Year. *Science,* December 2015, pg 1456.
6. Hutchinson CA, et al: Design and synthesis of a minimal bacterial genome. *Science*, 25 March, 2016.
7. Multiple articles and authors: Design of a synthetic yeast genome, and six other articles. *Science,* 10 March 2017, 1038-1050.
8. Baltimore D, et al: International Summit on Human Gene Editing, National Academy of Sciences, Washington, D.C., *Science* 348:36-38, 2015.
9. Lee M, Chan B, Clark PA: Deafness and prenatal testing: A case study analysis. Internet *J Family Practice*, 14: 1-7, 2016.

Contents

Preface

I t has been said that no new technology has ever gone unused. Clearly, the new technology of genetic engineering will be no exception. Already it is being utilized to change the genetic blueprint of bacteria, plants and some animals, and every advance is scrutinized for possible application in man. This new science is changing forever the way we think of life, not just at the molecular level, but at all levels of organization.

The intent of this book is to explore, in the format of a novel, the choices, as well as the lack of choice, that are presented by this exceptional biotechnology. As genetic engineering matures over the next years and decades, it will become feasible to engineer the genes of future generations of mankind with ever-increasing precision. While previous seminal advances in technology such as written language, mathematics, electricity, manned flight, nuclear energy, and the computer have all given man astounding and powerful new tools, it is genetic engineering that will give man, for the first time, the tools to redesign man himself.

Despite the extraordinarily high stakes, recognized in the National Institutes of Health's decision to publicly disseminate proposals for scientific research in this area, the national debate has, to this point, been limited and unfocused. It is hoped that this book will help inform members of the general public of the nature of genetic engineering and of its potential and probable uses so that the societal decisions, which eventually must be made, can be based on reason and understanding, and result in the greatest possible good.

Introductions

As I walked toward the dean's office I could feel myself becoming increasingly anxious, which only made me angry. It wasn't like I had done anything wrong. It was just that I was planning to do something a little different. I was sure that my intentions had reached the dean's office and had resulted in this summons.

After a brief wait in the outer office, Dr. Edwards, Dean of the Medical School, appeared.

"Please come in Bryan," he said in his usual pleasant but measured manner. After we were seated he continued, "Dr. Levitt tells me that you've decided not to take a residency next year. Is this true?"

Although I had rehearsed the answer many times in my head, it was still difficult to explain, probably because I wasn't sure of the logic myself.

"It's true," I started, trying to make it sound like the decision wasn't open for negotiation. "I've decided I need a break, that I need to do something different for a couple of years."

I had been totally and completely immersed in medicine and molecular genetics for almost six years (the time required for the combined MD/PhD program), not to mention premed for four years before that. I had even spent my summers doing research, and had always wondered what I'd missed. I was now finishing my thesis project with Dr. Stephen

Levitt, an internationally renowned molecular geneticist and, not incidentally, a recent Nobel laureate.

"I understand you are planning to work for the Brookings Institution?" Dean Edwards continued with an expression of disbelief.

"It will give me a broader perspective on things," I answered, "yet keep me in touch with medicine. It's a position as a research consultant in molecular genetics." I wanted to make it sound important, legitimate.

"It's not the sort of thing our graduates usually do, especially from the combined program," he asserted. "I'm aware that your research for your thesis is going very well. We naturally assumed that you would complete a residency and take a position in academic medicine. Or at least go straight into research."

"I still plan to do that," I countered.

"But you must know that it's hard to drop out for a couple of years and then get back in as if you'd never been away," Dean Edwards persisted, somewhat impatiently.

"I know, but I think I can do it," I said, bringing us to an uncomfortable impasse.

"Well, think about it carefully," he finished, getting up to signal the end of the conversation.

"Thanks for discussing it with me," I said perfunctorily.

"Well, did you do it?" asked Anne as I entered our apartment.

"Did I do what?" I replied, knowing pretty well what she meant.

"Stick to your guns with the dean. You did have your meeting didn't you?" she queried.

"He did make me feel a bit guilty. He as much as said that I was deserting the noble cause of biomedical research, but we're still heading for Washington," I said.

"He didn't threaten to take your name off the Cornell and Rockefeller alumni rolls?" she teased. (My combined degree program was a medical degree from Cornell Medical College and a PhD from Rockefeller University. The two institutions occupy conveniently adjacent sites along York Avenue on the East Side of Manhattan.)

"Actually, I'm really looking forward to a more armchair job. Lab work is kind of messy." We had discussed the decision ad nauseam.

"You just don't want to get up in the middle of the night," she went on.

It was true. The thing I hated most about my clinical rotations in medical school was those 3:00 a.m. phone calls that meant getting up, going to the hospital, working through some emergency, and then being dead tired the next day. I'm not sure which is worse, getting up in the middle of the night or being so exhausted the next day. And what made it even worse was that Anne, now in her last year of pediatric residency, had lots of night call. Every third night she slept in the hospital. In addition, she was on call at home another third night. Simple arithmetic meant that she had one night to recover before starting again. This had been the routine for our two years of married life since graduating together from med school.

"Well, your research job next year will give you a reasonable schedule," I replied to Anne's unstated comparison of her schedule to mine. Anne had obtained a prized research position at the National Institutes of Health, or NIH as it is known, in Bethesda, just across the Potomac from Washington, DC. It involved no direct clinical responsibility, which meant no night call. However, I should emphasize that the position was prized for the research opportunities, not the lack of night call.

On the other hand the Brookings Institution, and my job, were clearly not prized, at least not among members of the biomedical research community.

Lecture to the Medical Students — Genetics I

Things in the lab were going tremendously. They usually did in Dr. Levitt's lab. He was considered one of the fathers of genetic engineering (the technology used to add or delete genes to or from cells). Members of his lab had just gotten seven scientific abstracts accepted for presentation at the upcoming annual meeting of the American Society for Molecular Genetics. I was a coauthor on three of them and principal author on one – the one I would present. This would give me the opportunity to present my PhD research, two years' worth of effort, to all of the most distinguished molecular geneticists.

My research involved transferring whole genomes (the entire DNA or genetic material of a cell) from one cell to another, specifically from a somatic or body cell to an ovum or egg cell. The goal was straightforward: to allow cloning of desirable genomes. At present, cloning could only be accomplished by splitting the cells of very early embryos, the same way that identical twins are formed. But, in the case of identical twins, only a limited number of "copies" can be made, and their traits or talents are not apparent until later when no additional copies can be created.

If the entire genetic material from adult somatic cells could be transferred into an ovum whose nucleus (containing the ovum's genetic material) had been removed, and if the ovum would then develop, unlimited copies of an individual with desirable traits could be produced. To date this process had not worked; the genome in adult cells apparently differentiates and loses the capacity to form an entire individual even though the complete set of genes is present. The challenge was to reverse this differentiation. And, of course, the technique would only be applied to plants and animals, not man. Until now researchers had succeeded in transplanting only small amounts of DNA or genes from one cell to another.

When I had told Dr. Levitt of my decision to leave mainstream molecular genetics for a couple of years, he had been moderately understanding, all things considered. After initial disbelief and an attempt to change my mind, our relationship was back to the usual friendly, but businesslike, approach as before. However, I knew his private thoughts would be to doubt my intellectual commitment. He probably attributed this lack of dedication to my medical degree; meaning a pure "PhD" certainly wouldn't stray from the research path.

It was now quarter to eleven, time to head over to the main lecture hall at the medical school across the street. For the last couple of years I had given a two-lecture overview of molecular genetics and its clinical implications to the first year medical students. These were the only lectures to medical students that I gave all year. They always made me a little nervous. It was much easier talking about my own research to peers at seminars or research meetings. Then, since it was my own work, I could count on knowing more about the subject than anyone else, and the audience would, in general, be sympathetic to the limitations and weaknesses of the field since they worked in the same specialty area. But in this lecture, I covered a large amount of ground and was always waiting for some obnoxious first-year medical student who had majored in biochemistry or embryology (areas that I touched on briefly) to catch me on something or to ask some pointed question casting doubt on the importance of the whole subject.

After waiting a few minutes for everyone to get settled (there were about eighty-five students in the class), I introduced myself and explained that the purpose of the lectures was to give them an overview of molecular and medical genetics. I indicated that it was an interruptible talk if they had any questions, and that they would not need to take notes as they would have detailed courses on this material next semester. (However, I knew there would be a few who would feel compelled to take copious notes anyway, a reliable way to identify those who were excessively obsessive-compulsive.)

"If we look back over history," I began, "our generation is really the first to have a reasonably complete understanding of human reproduction and genetics. One of the earliest recorded theories of reproduction was proposed by Aristotle in the third century BC. He suggested that semen originated in the man's blood and possessed the ability to form a viable embryo within the uterus by coagulating menstrual blood. Incredible as it may seem today, this concept was generally accepted for nearly two thousand years. Then in the seventeenth century, William Harvey demonstrated, by killing deer at various times after impregnation, that there never was evidence for coagulation of menstrual blood. Instead, a small embryo appeared within the uterus and gradually developed and enlarged during gestation. A fanciful depiction of the thinking of those times is shown in this first slide of a homunculus within a sperm. Implicit in this drawing is that the male parent contributed the entire genetic blueprint of the new individual."

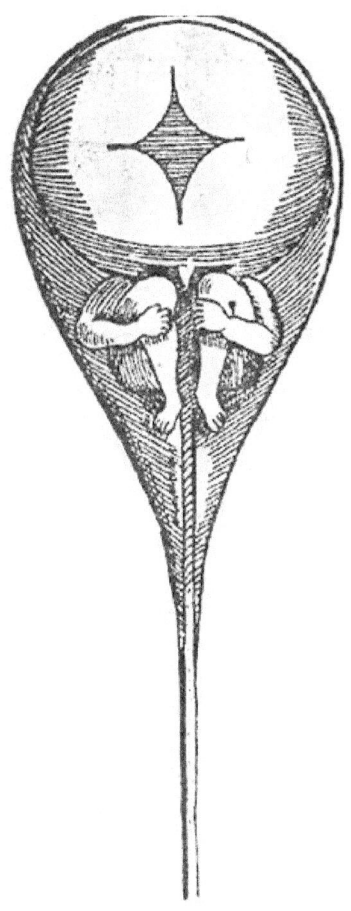

This last statement and slide were greeted by the predictable female hissing.

"Later in the seventeenth century the Dutch scientist Regnier de Graaf discovered that the fundamental event in conception is the union of the sperm and egg or ovum. His discovery resulted from observations in mammals of small cysts on the ovaries which would release ova. These small predominantly fluid-filled cysts are now known in his honor as Graafian follicles. This discovery led naturally to the idea that both parents contributed to the transmitted characteristics of the offspring, a concept that was resisted for many years.

"The great contribution of Gregor Mendel, the Moravian monk, was to apply quantitative and statistical methods to the expression of inherited traits through several generations. Working in the latter half of the nineteenth century in Brno, Czech Republic, Mendel studied a number of pairs of contrasting characteristics in the ordinary garden pea. These characteristics included traits such as height: tall versus dwarf; color: green versus yellow; seed texture: smooth versus wrinkled; and so forth. Working with one trait at a time, he crossed parents possessing opposite traits and noted the frequency of the traits in the offspring. In the first generation of offspring only one trait was expressed, in the case of height all the offspring of a cross between tall and dwarf parents were tall. Therefore, the trait 'tall' was dominant and the trait 'dwarf' was recessive.

"Even more interesting were the results from self-pollinating the hybrids, for example, the offspring obtained from the tall/dwarf cross. Some of the new offspring were tall and some were dwarf. And the ratio of the dominant trait 'tall' to the recessive trait 'dwarf' was approximately 3:1. Mendel realized that the results were consistent with each trait being represented by two factors in each individual, one contributed from each of the two parents. Thus, of the three tall offspring in the second generation, one offspring would have two factors for tallness and two offspring would have one factor each for tallness, and one offspring would have two factors for dwarfness. These findings can be summarized in a so-called Punnett's square as shown in the second slide. Here the capital 'T' symbolizes the tall gene, and the small 't' the dwarf gene. These hereditary factors, which code for tall or dwarf stature of an individual, are referred to as the genotype and the expression of these factors, i.e. the appearance and behavior, as the phenotype. Thus, the pea plants with two factors for tall and the plants with one factor for tall and one for dwarf would have different genotypes but the same phenotypes.

Punnett's Square

Male genes

	T	t
T	T T	t T
t	T t	t t

Female genes

"It is interesting to note that Mendel's published results have been shown to be too good! That is, from a statistical point of view, his results match the theoretical too closely. This evidence of falsification has been graciously explained by suggesting that Mendel was trying to demonstrate his theory rather than to simply conduct an experiment to test a hypothesis. More likely, Mendel didn't understand probability and thought that the results from small numbers of experiments should match those predicted for a large number, and when they didn't, he simply adjusted them. In any event the validity of Mendel's theory has been confirmed numerous times and is now the basis of all genetic theory.

"With confirmation of Mendel's theory of inheritance, there was intense interest in determining the underlying physical basis of heredity.

It was well established that all plants and animals were composed of microscopic cells and the products of those cells, and that within every cell were threadlike structures called chromosomes. In 1903 the chromosomal theory of inheritance was proposed independently by Theodor Boveri and Walter S. Sutton. Previously, the association between the hereditary factors of Mendel, i.e. genes and chromosomes, had not been appreciated. The behavior of the chromosomes at the time of cell division would explain Mendelian inheritance. Their behavior during cell division in reproductive cells is compared to their behavior in non-reproductive cells in the third slide; you'll study this process in detail later.

Duplication of Chromosomes in Cell Division

Mitosis (Somatic cells)	Meiosis (Reproductive cells)

One pair of chromosomes — One pair of chromosomes

Duplication of chromosomes — Duplication of chromosomes

Chromosomes separate individually — Chromosomes separate as pairs

Daughter cells with chromosomes identical to parent cell — Daughter cells with different chromosomes from parent cell

Reproductive cells with half the chromosomes of parent cell

"Interestingly, Sutton proposed his theory while still a medical student. He then became a surgeon and never returned to the field that made him famous."

I resisted the temptation to make the standard derogatory remark about surgery and those who go into it, partly because I was sure Dr. Levitt would see similarities between this well-known anecdote and my decision to leave research, even if only temporarily. And my contributions, at least to date, were orders of magnitude below Sutton's.

"At this point the focus of investigation turned to the questions of how genetic information was contained within the chromosomes and how this information was expressed in terms of enzyme formation, protein synthesis, and cell growth and division. Although many scientists contributed significantly to unraveling the genetic code, the contribution that stands out above all others is the discovery of the structure of DNA, or deoxyribonucleic acid, by M. H. F. Wilkins, F. H. C. Crick, and J. D. Watson in 1953. The DNA structure is shown at the top of the last slide.

"As you can see each chromosome contains two very long strands of DNA in the form of a double helix. That is, each chromosome is made up of two strands of nucleotide bases, which are wound around each other. The strands are chemically joined where each pair of nucleotides meets.

"This discovery, based on x-ray diffraction studies, elucidated the interrelationship of the four nucleic acids of DNA and explained both how different combinations of the four nucleic acids could code for all of the twenty amino acids found in proteins, and how DNA and the genetic material it contained could be faithfully reproduced at the time of cell division. For this achievement they were awarded the Nobel Prize in 1962.

"At the bottom of the last slide the process of DNA replication or reproduction is depicted. The daughter chromosomes are clones of the parent. The two nucleotide strands of the parent separate; then each

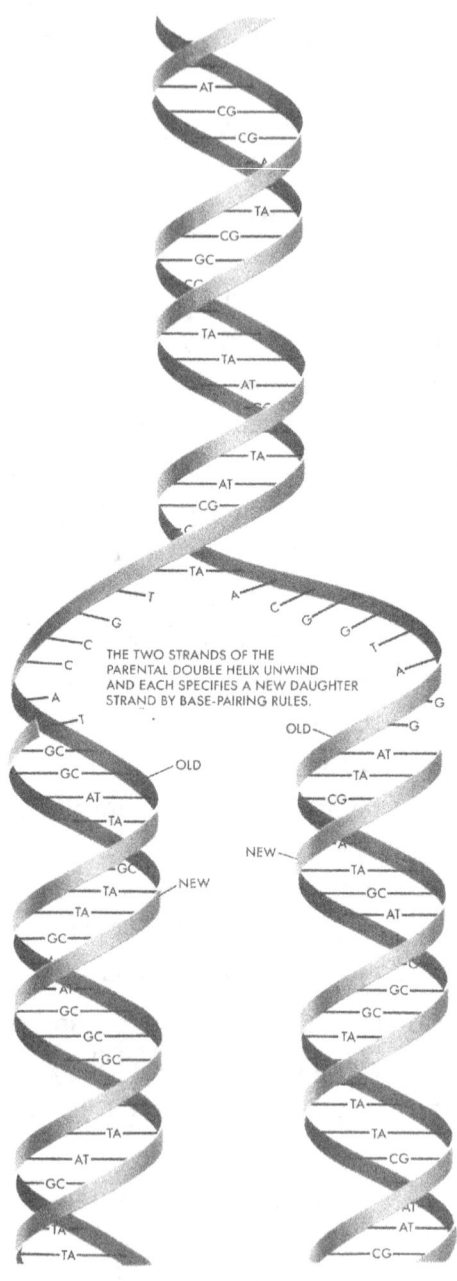

THE TWO STRANDS OF THE
PARENTAL DOUBLE HELIX UNWIND
AND EACH SPECIFIES A NEW DAUGHTER
STRAND BY BASE-PAIRING RULES.

strand combines with a set of complementary nucleotides so that two chromosomes, each consisting of two strands, are formed. The two daughter chromosomes are identical to each other and the parent.

"The great diversity of proteins and compounds found in living cells are all coded for by the linear sequence of nucleotides in the DNA. Various sequences of three nucleotides code for the amino acids, which in turn are the building blocks for proteins. Only three nucleotides are required since there are sixty-four different sequences possible with four different nucleotides to choose from for each of the three positions, i.e., four times four times four. The average gene contains approximately one thousand nucleotides and codes for a single protein, and the human genome contains approximately twenty-seven thousand genes.

"The next important step toward recombinant DNA technology or genetic engineering was the discovery in 1970 of so-called 'restriction enzymes' by Hamilton and Smith at Johns Hopkins. These enzymes, and similar ones discovered later, allow strands of DNA to be cut and spliced at precise chemical locations. For this discovery Hamilton and Smith were awarded the 1978 Nobel Prize.

"For the purpose of this introductory talk, I will skip what is known concerning the important processes of gene control, i.e., turning genes on and off and regulating the amount of protein that is produced by a gene. Progress in these areas of research has already produced several additional Nobel prizes in the field of genetics and more are sure to follow.

"In the second talk we will focus on the human and medical aspects of genetics. Are there any questions on the material covered today?" I asked.

"How far off is genetic therapy for human disease?" asked one particularly aggressive-looking medical student, the type that has to ask a question at the end of every lecture, no matter whether he already knows the answer.

"To date," I answered, "there have been two unsuccessful attempts at genetic therapy for enzyme deficiencies of cells of the bone marrow. In both cases, cells from the patient's own bone marrow were harvested by biopsy. Then the gene that coded for the enzyme that the patient lacked was inserted into the harvested cells using a virus vector. After biochemically confirming that the inserted gene was functional, the cells were then injected back into the patient. In both cases, there was never any evidence that the missing enzyme functioned in the recipient; presumably, the reinjected cells never propagated to the extent that they could produce significant amounts of the transplanted enzyme.

"Since these experiments, one of which was in Italy, the NIH has issued strict gene therapy guidelines. Specifically, the Working Group on Human Gene Therapy, a subcommittee of the NIH Recombinant DNA Advisory Committee, has stated that, one, there must be open public access to future proposals for human gene therapy, two, for the present only somatic (non-reproductive) cell therapy will be considered, and, three, patients must agree to long term follow-up including an autopsy at the time of death as a condition of participation in the study. I think you can see from these three requirements that the NIH attaches the greatest possible importance to this area of research, particularly as it relates to the general public and changes in the gene pool. We will discuss these developments more in the next lecture."

The aggressive-looking student looked satisfied that his question had dealt with such an important and controversial area.

3

The Problem

"How was your talk today?" Anne asked as she finished dressing, probably trying to take my mind off the fact that we were late. We had tickets for the philharmonic that night.

"Brilliant, of course," I replied. "The medical students are definitely becoming attuned to genetic engineering. It used to be you never got any questions or much interest in the subject. Now I think it is becoming clear to everyone, even medical students, that genetic engineering in humans is a technology whose time has come."

In the cab on the way to Lincoln Center Anne recounted a particularly sad experience she had in clinic that day. It had fallen to her to inform a couple that their two-year-old daughter had Hurler's disease or gargoylism, its older name. This genetically transmitted disease causes progressive disfigurement of the face and body leading to death over several years. The parents knew only too well of all the details having been through this tragedy with a young son several years before. Hurler's disease is inherited as an autosomal recessive, which means that both parents must be carriers of the defective gene. Each child will have a one-fourth chance of inheriting the defective gene from both parents and thus of having the disease. Those children who inherit only one defective gene will not manifest the disease, but will be carriers like their parents.

"When are you molecular geneticists going to come up with a cure for Hurler's?" Anne asked half-facetiously. Clinicians, physicians like Anne who take care of patients, are always impatiently waiting for advances from the biomedical researchers, who, like myself, spend most of their time in the lab doing benchtop research.

"Unfortunately, probably not too soon," I replied.

As Anne was fully aware, Hurler's is caused by an enzyme defect that results in the abnormal metabolism of certain substances in a variety of cells. The cells become stuffed with the non-metabolized material. The trick is to get the missing enzyme into the body's cells; a simple intravenous injection of the enzyme doesn't work.

"What we need," I continued, "is a harmless virus that the normal gene for the enzyme can be attached to. Then we can infect the patient and let the virus enter the patient's cells and insert the good gene into the patients DNA."

Progress in this direction was being made, but there were substantial biological problems yet to be solved. Viruses naturally enter living cells and insert their own genetic material into the host cells fooling the host cell into producing more viruses. However, viruses have to be found that infect those cells in the body that require the enzyme in question but don't destroy the host cell at the end of the process.

We arrived at Avery Fischer Hall amid the usual last-minute rush. It's ironic how the same people who elbow their way through the crowds behave in such a civilized manner once inside and seated.

The symphony has always been my favorite among the performing arts. Music by itself, without the visual cues of elaborate sets and moving performers, allows more mental freedom. With singing, acting, and dancing the mind is much more directed.

After the symphony we stopped at our favorite East Side Italian bistro for a late dinner. The subject turned again to genetic engineering.

"I don't know about genetic engineering in people. It's hard to imagine," Anne commented. "It goes against every culture that's ever existed."

"It would definitely be the ultimate step in the biomedical revolution," I replied, "but I can't think of any technology that's ever been developed and never used, so I guess this one will be used, too."

"It clearly could make a big impact on disease," Anne mused. "One out of twenty pediatric admissions is for a purely genetic disease. And I'm sure an even larger percentage are conditioned or worsened by one's genes."

In fact, thirteen hundred documented genetic diseases have been catalogued in man to date, and these are the easy ones.

"Think of the savings in money and suffering if you could just eliminate the genes that code for the appendix and gallbladder!" I said, impressed with my own thought. "Neither serve any necessary function yet inflammation of these two vestigial organs alone represents two of the most common indications for surgery."

"Having a genetically engineered kid would be a little like adopting except that you would get to pick the genome," Anne went on. "Not only would you know whether it was going to be a boy or a girl, but what it would look like, what its talents would be, what its personality would be like, et cetera."

"And then you would find out that all the neighborhood women had picked the same genome!" I interjected. "Definitely worse than buying the same dress."

"It seems to me that people will never go for genetically engineered kids. They're too chauvinistic about their own genes," Anne reflected. "That's coded into their genes, too."

"What about the competitive factor though? It may force people to decide otherwise," I said. "Imagine if your neighbors were selecting all these genomes guaranteed to produce super humans and your natural kids were going to have to compete against them. And, the competitive pressures wouldn't be just the neighborhood, they would be national and international as well."

"Sure, but the basic problem is, who's going to select the genomes?" Anne replied. "If individuals do it, the country will have a surplus of movie stars and not enough scientists, and nobody will want the government doing it for them."

"That's clearly the key problem," I agreed. "It's going to be a huge national debate. It'll dominate the media, politics, and supermarket magazines for years."

"I think it's time to get home so I can get some sleep. It's my night off," Anne interrupted.

"Right, we need to keep our natural skills up just in case science fails us," I added as Anne gave me one of those 'oh, how crude' looks.

4

Lecture to the Medical Students — Genetics II

" In the last talk," I began, "we reviewed the important discoveries in genetics that have led to our present state of knowledge. We saw how the genetic code resides in the chemical structure of chromosomes and how genes are passed from one generation to the next. Today we will focus on human genetics and its medical implications."

This would be my last lecture to the medical school students before leaving for Washington, DC and the Brookings Institution, and it gave me an urge to be sweeping and eloquent although I rarely managed either.

"We've seen how genes code for all the enzymes of the body, which in turn, determine the structure and chemistry of the body. However, one's environment also plays a role. A clear example of the influence of environment is in the language we speak. If a child of German parents is raised in France by French parents, he will, of course, speak French in spite of his German genes.

"The relative influence of genes and environment in determining behavior is an area of longstanding controversy. To study this question rigorously one must have either individuals with different genomes raised in identical environments or individuals with identical genomes raised in different environments. While the fact that two individuals are raised in the same family means that many environmental factors are similar, it does not mean that they are identical. For instance, the firstborn son will be treated differently from the son who is the youngest of five in the same family.

"On the other hand, identical twins will by definition have the same genomes. While there might be some differences in the environments of identical twins raised in the same family, these differences are too small and too difficult to document to give us significant environmental variables to study. However, occasionally identical twins are separated at birth and reared in quite different environments. This situation provides a unique opportunity to study the effect of environmental factors."

I was leading up to a very unusual study of the relative effects of nature and nurture.

"Recently," I continued, "a group of researchers at the University of Minnesota undertook a project to identify and study identical twins who were separated at birth and reared apart. The results from nine such pairs have been reported in the journal *Science*. The similarities in personality and behavioral traits between twins, despite the fact that some were raised in very different circumstances, were striking.

"One pair of male twins was born in Trinidad to a Jewish father and a German mother. Shortly after birth the mother took one twin back to Germany where he was raised as a Catholic and a Nazi youth by his grandmother; the other was raised in the Caribbean as a Jew by his father and spent part of his youth in a kibbutz. The two men, forty-seven years old when interviewed, led quite different lives: the German was an industrial supervisor in Germany, was married, and was a loyal union man while the other ran a retail clothing store in San Diego, was separated, and was a workaholic. However, there were many striking similarities. They both liked spicy foods and sweet liqueurs, were absentminded, had a habit of falling asleep in front of the television set, thought it was funny to sneeze in a crowd of strangers, flushed the toilet before using it, stored rubber bands on their wrists, and read magazines from back to front! In addition, both are domineering toward women despite the fact that one was raised by a woman and the other by a man.

"In general, the other pairs of identical twins reared apart also showed amazing similarities. One pair had similar histories of endogenous depression. Another pair had virtually identical patterns of headaches including onset at age eighteen, occurrence in late afternoon, and use of the same words to describe the pain. Many of these similarities, if found in identical twins raised together, would previously have been attributed to similar environments.

"Now that we have seen the importance of genes in determining not only physical and physiologic characteristics, but also behavioral traits, let's very briefly touch on another area that has been revolutionized by our current knowledge of molecular genetics and the techniques of genetic engineering. That area is the field of evolution, particularly human evolution. The field of evolution studies the causes of the appearance of new genes and factors that determine the abundance of a given gene in the population.

"New genes occur because of mutations, that is changes in the chemical structure of the DNA which makes up our genes. These changes can be induced by toxic chemicals, but are thought to result primarily from radiation from cosmic rays. Cosmic rays from outer space interact in our atmosphere to produce gamma rays that are constantly passing through all of us. Usually, no adverse effect occurs, but occasionally a mutation is produced in an ovum or sperm or their precursors. Since these mutations cause random chemical changes, most mutations are deleterious, that is they do not improve on existing genes which have survived the selective pressures of time.

"The techniques of molecular genetics have allowed us to reexamine the evolution of homo sapiens both with respect to his origins and the time of appearance of what we recognize as modern man. Molecular genetics has allowed us to refine the answers to these questions by allowing us to match the nucleotide or chemical makeup of human genes to those of other primates.

"These efforts," I went on, "show that, in general, there is great similarity, chemically, between the genes of man and the genes of primates. In addition, there is greater similarity between man's genes and the African apes than to apes from other parts of the world. This provides additional evidence for the African origin of homo sapiens. The greatest genetic similarity is with the chimpanzee; approximately ninety-eight percent of the genes are identical, establishing this clown of the animal kingdom as man's closest living relative.

"Another finding attributable to advances in molecular genetics has allowed us to improve our estimate of the time of appearance of man. The regular occurrence of mutations in the so-called junk DNA or non-functional DNA of our chromosomes provides a sort of genetic clock. The current estimate is that man, in the form we know today, arose between 100,000 and 200,000 years ago in Africa.

"What factors lead to a given gene becoming dominant in a population or becoming extinct? The abundance of a gene in the population can, on one level, be thought of as being secondary to selective pressures in the Darwinian sense. That is, a gene that causes the death of an individual prior to the reproductive years will not 'live' to reproduce itself. However, on another level, if people with subnormal, but nonlethal, genes have more children than those with above-normal genes then there will be a gradual decline in gene quality.

"Ironically, a modern-day factor that contributes to a decline in the quality of the gene pool, and in that sense, the quality of future generations, is medical care. The bleeding disorder hemophilia A is an examples of this phenomenon. The disease is X-linked meaning that the abnormal gene is on the X chromosome. Since only one normal gene is needed for normal blood clotting, females can be carriers, but rarely manifest the disease. Males, who only have one X chromosome, will manifest the disease if their one X chromosome carries the abnormal gene for hemophilia. Without periodic injections of replacement clotting factors these individuals would not live to reproductive age. It would, of course, be unethical to withhold treatment in these situations in an effort to improve the gene pool.

"I'd like to spend the last few minutes looking at the future of human genetics," I continued. This would be purely speculative and normally wouldn't be included, but this lecture was not part of a formal course. Besides it was my last lecture at Cornell.

"We now have the ability to map the genes of the human chromosomes, that is, to determine their location on the chromosomes and their chemical composition. This work is well underway, but there are many unanswered questions. At the same time the cost and speed for sequencing the entire human genome has decreased dramatically.

"Other techniques have been developed that allow the injection of artificial genes into a cell. This is accomplished by attaching the gene to a suitable virus that carries the gene into a cell and inserts the gene into the cell's DNA. In the case of somatic or non-reproductive cells, the new gene will affect the products or function of only that cell and its descendants within the original individual.

"A landmark experiment has been done in which the gene responsible for the production of growth hormone in the rat was inserted into a fertilized reproductive cell of a mouse. The cell was then implanted into a mouse uterus where it was allowed to mature. After birth, as you can see from this slide, the animal resembled a normal mouse in every way except that it grew to be the size of a rat. The other mouse is a sibling that did not receive the rat growth hormone gene. This experiment is interesting not only because of the fact that it was a technical success, but also because it demonstrated, as expected, that genes themselves are not species specific."

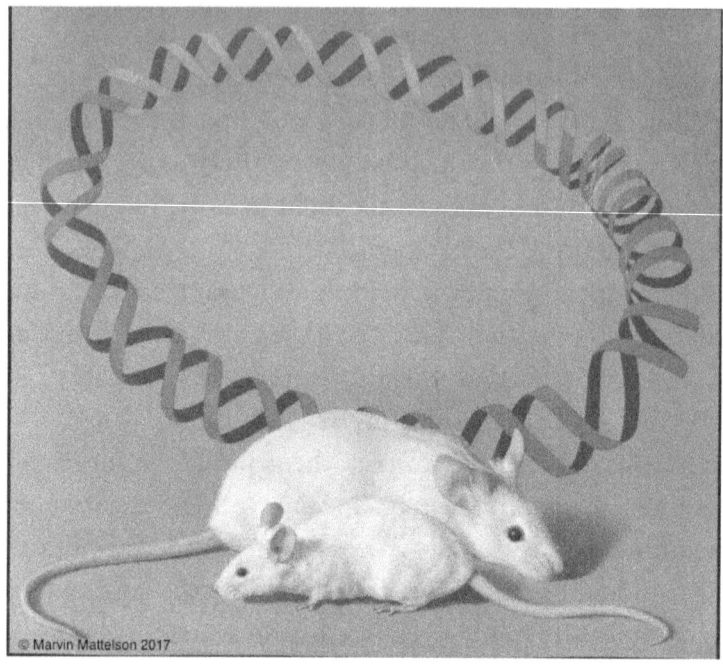

© Marvin Mattelson 2017

I concluded with a few thoughts on where this powerful new technology might lead us.

"Eventually we may find that we have the technology to reliably and easily reproduce genomes, that is cloning, or to design new desirable genomes, or 'designer genes' as some have called them, by mixing the best genes from multiple individuals. This ability could have a tremendous impact on the disease spectrum. Genetic disease would be eliminated. Medical genetics may very well become the preventive medicine of the future. Genetic engineering could eliminate genetic diseases in one or two generations similar to the manner in which vaccines have eliminated or controlled many infectious diseases.

"Obviously there are significant medical and even larger social risks in such undertakings. I think that in the case of genetic engineering, society through its representative, the federal government, will be involved in deciding what therapies are appropriate to a greater extent than ever before.

"In the few remaining minutes, I would be happy to answer any questions," I offered.

A bookish-looking student in the front row raised his hand. "How will we be sure in advance what the effect of a given gene will be?"

"Well, in general, we will know mainly from previous experience," I answered. "In the case of reproducing an entire genome we can assume that the new individual will be as similar to the previous 'model' as one identical twin is to another."

"What about mixing genes from several individuals to make a new genome?" he asked before I could get to that point.

"There will certainly be an unknown element in that situation," I responded. "But it will be similar to the current 'natural' situation. Especially when you consider that we all have no idea what recessive genes we carry. There is clearly a large element of chance in natural reproduction."

"Who will decide what genes or genomes are available to which couples?" asked a serious-looking female medical student.

"That's a very good question," I replied. "It will clearly be a new level of complexity and responsibility for the FDA. Unfortunately, I do think some degree of centralized control or planning will be needed. Otherwise, we might end up with an excess of rockstars and not enough engineers. That question will need to be extensively and thoroughly debated by society in the years to come. The decisions will have the most far-reaching consequences for society as well as for the individual."

5

Senate Hearing

As we drove across the George Washington Bridge, I had that same feeling I had had on graduating from prep school and college. Graduation gives you tangible evidence of accomplishment with no immediate responsibilities and, for the moment, no possibility of failures related to the next undertaking.

Being a sunny summer day and having the top down certainly contributed to the feeling. While Anne and I were both excited about the prospect of living in Washington, DC for a while, we knew we would miss the finer cultural offerings of New York. But the crowds, dirt, and unfriendliness of New York City (from which we were mostly isolated at the medical center) would not be missed.

"One thing about New York, it sure gives you a great look at the variety in the current gene pool," I commented. "Probably just about every gene on this planet is represented there."

"And there's clearly a lot of room for improvement, even aside from genetic disease," Anne replied as we both conjured up thoughts of various New York scenes in which abnormal as well as suboptimal genes were clearly manifest. The masses of New York humanity always seemed to provide living proof of the limitations of genetic selection through evolution alone. It was easy to speak so irreverently now that we were safely in New Jersey.

"Did you see the article in *The Times* that the Senate is considering holding hearings on genetic engineering?" I asked.

"No," Anne answered. "You mean the human type?"

"Yeah, and it'll be televised," I went on. "Should be better than the Watergate hearings."

To date, those in the biomedical community had been struck by the relative lack of public interest in the first tentative steps toward human genetic engineering and in the debate in the scientific community over the proposed guidelines for research in this area. Televised Senate hearings on these questions could certainly change that. As we followed the interstate south I tried to imagine what these hearings might be like.

"Good evening, I'm Phil Brubaker. Tonight Cable Network will be broadcasting major portions of the first day of Senate hearings on genetic engineering in humans. These hearings are being held by the Senate Committee on Health and Human Services chaired by Senator Samuel Smathers of Illinois. One of the main functions of this committee is to oversee the National Institutes of Health, usually referred to as the NIH. By funding the majority of biomedical research in this country, the NIH can set guidelines and policies that determine what kind of research can be performed and in what manner. Although biomedical researchers are free to ignore NIH guidelines if their funding comes from other sources, they usually would not do so. In addition, these hearings may very well lead to congressional legislation which would then apply to all biomedical research in this country."

The TV image widened to include two additional people. "With me tonight are Milly Doland, Cable Network's science reporter for Capitol Hill, and Dr. Henry Levitt, an internationally known molecular geneticist from Rockefeller University in New York, who is going to help us with the technical side of the issues."

"Milly, let me begin with you," the announcer continued. "Can you give us the background of these hearings?"

"Yes, Phil," Ms. Doland replied as her face expanded to fill the screen. "The subject of genetic engineering has come up in the Senate before, but the difference this time is that the technology is now much further along. Genetic engineering in humans is no longer just a theoretical possibility in the future, but on some levels is already feasible. There are some members of this Committee, such as Senator Winston Dillon of South Carolina, who are known to feel strongly that Congress should pass legislation to regulate genetic engineering in humans. It is also no secret that Senator Dillon thinks that this legislation should effectively prohibit all genetic engineering in humans. On the other hand, there is Senator Robert Hardiway of California who is thought to favor proceeding in this area in a carefully controlled manner. The other three members of the committee have no known positions on genetic engineering in humans. They are: Senator William Smathers of Illinois, the Committee Chairman, Senator Richard Wong of Hawaii, and Senator Dominic Allesio of Massachusetts."

"Thank you, Milly," Phil Brubaker interjected. "Dr. Levitt, I want to thank you for joining us. I'm sure your comments will be invaluable to our listeners in understanding the technical aspects of genetic engineering. Would you give us a brief overview of genetic engineering?"

I couldn't help but be amused at the similarity of my mentor's situation to pro athletes who are always present to provide expert commentary for televised sports events. However, the similarity ended with the setting; Dr. Levitt's dignified demeanor and scientific approach set him apart from the usual television fare.

"Phil, let me start by reviewing very briefly some of the basics of heredity. The reason species breed true, that is that dogs reproduce dogs and maple trees reproduce maple trees, is that all living things contain a blueprint for that organism consisting of chemical substances called genes. In the case of man there are over twenty-seven thousand genes making up this blueprint. Although each cell contains a complete blueprint, it will only use or express that part of the blueprint that it needs for its particular function within the body.

"Genes for a given purpose," Dr. Levitt continued using various visual aids, "like eye color, come in various forms, which explains why some individuals have blue eyes and others have brown eyes. The control of the genetic blueprint over the final product is quite extensive and is a major determinant of intelligence and personality as well as the more easily seen physical attributes, such as eye color.

"Genetic engineering in humans, also known as human gene therapy, falls into two categories," he added. "First there is somatic gene therapy which involves correcting a genetic defect in an existing individual. The correction is done in the non-reproductive cells, called somatic cells, of the body and, therefore, the genetic change cannot be passed on to the individual's offspring. Attempts at this kind of gene therapy are already being tried. The second type of human gene therapy involves changes in genes in reproductive cells. These changes would be passed on to future generations and changes of this type have the potential to significantly change the genetic composition of the human race. For this reason this type of genetic engineering is quite controversial and to date no experiments of this type have been conducted in humans."

"Dr. Levitt, can you comment on the relative lack of public interest in or awareness of this technology?" Phil Brubaker asked.

"To date the possibility of significant change in human genes has been only an abstract idea. There has been no actual example, no living proof, so to speak, of this technology for the public to see. A fair analogy might be our sending a man to the moon. The theoretical possibility and technical capability was there for years before the actual event. In fact, thousands of researchers worked for years preparing for the event. Yet the average American was relatively startled and overwhelmed when they actually saw, on their television screens, a man walk on the moon. The same is true of genetic engineering in humans," Dr. Levitt replied.

"Thank you, Dr. Levitt. We will now go to the Senate hearings live from Capitol Hill," Phil Brubaker announced.

The television screen showed an ornate Senate hearing room. The five senators were seated behind the raised bench with their aides, mostly rather young looking, seated or standing behind them. In the audience were those who were to testify, various interested parties, habitual hearing attendees, and members of the media.

"The purpose of these hearings," began Senator Smathers, a distinguished-looking gentleman wearing reading glasses, "is to take public testimony on the question of whether Congress should pass legislation regulating research in and the practice of human gene therapy. Normally, questions of the propriety of medical research are resolved within the National Institutes of Health and questions of the practice of medical therapy would be the responsibility of the Food and Drug Administration. However, in the case of human gene therapy we are dealing with a form of technology which, in some forms, will not only affect consenting individuals, but will affect the genetic constitution of future generations of Americans.

"Counsel, please call the first witness," Senator Smathers went on.

"Will Mr. Clyde Hamilton take the witness seat?" requested the chief lawyer for the committee. A mildly overweight middle-aged man wearing a plaid polyester suit rose and took the witness seat.

"Please state your name, place of residence, and affiliation," the committee lawyer continued.

"Yes sir, my name is Clyde Hamilton from Purdy, Missouri and I'm the president of the Missouri Right to Life chapter," the man stated with great earnestness.

"Do you have an initial statement Mr. Hamilton?" asked Senator Smathers.

"Yes, Senator," replied Mr. Hamilton. "We in the Right to Life movement firmly believe that tampering with human genes is unnatural and immoral. God created life, and it is not the place of man to alter it any more than it is permissible for man to cause the abortion of unborn living fetuses. To allow research to progress in the area of human genetic engineering will inevitably lead to a misuse of this technology. For instance, we see the cloning of individuals as a very likely consequence of genetic engineering; I don't think any of us wants that. We feel that other approaches to the treatment of disease that do not involve tampering with an individual's genes are or will be sufficient."

"I don't mean to imply that I disagree with you," said Senator Smathers, "but could you elaborate on why you are against cloning?"

"We see it as the most vulgar form of genetic engineering, Senator," Mr. Hamilton explained. "God creates each of us as a unique individual. He does not mean for human beings to be made in mass production like on an assembly line."

"How do you view identical twins or identical triplets?" Senator Smathers went on.

"Those are rare occurrences, and the identical individuals are in the same family. In addition, these individuals experience life without knowledge of their potential or limitations just like the rest of us. With cloning there would be individuals who had lived before, with the same identical genes, and the cloned individual would know his fate in advance," Mr. Hamilton responded, apparently pleased with his last point.

"Senator Hardiway, I believe you had a question?" asked Senator Smathers.

"Yes, thank you," said Senator Hardiway. "Mr. Hamilton, I understand your reservations with respect to cloning, but why would you prohibit gene therapy for individuals with genetic disease for whom there was no alternative therapy?"

"Senator, this is the difficult side of the question of human genetic engineering," replied Mr. Hamilton. "Our fear is that if research is allowed to progress in one area of genetic engineering, it will inevitably lead to the utilization of these techniques in the more morally reprehensible areas as well. In addition, it is our view that the unfortunate state of those afflicted with a genetic disease is part of God's overall plan even though, at the time, we mortals are not able to discern His purpose."

"Do you have any objection to genetic engineering in animals and plants?" Senator Hardiway asked.

"Yes, Senator," answered Mr. Hamilton. "The Bible teaches us that God created the plants and animals, as well as man, and that it was good. It would be very presumptuous of man to think that he can do better."

"Mr. Hamilton," Senator Hardiway continued somewhat impatiently, "in my reading of the Bible I find no proscription against the development and use of man-made technology, only a proscription against its immoral use. While genetic engineering in humans certainly has the potential for undesirable consequences, so did the domestication of fire. It seems to me that genetic engineering has the potential for phenomenal benefits, including the elimination of a large percentage of human disease, a great increase in scientific and artistic talent, the enhancement of literally all aspects of human life and endeavor. If I may quote President Kennedy, 'God's work on earth must truly be our own.'"

"Senator Dillon, you wish to make a comment?" interjected Senator Smathers. Senator Dillon, an older white-haired man who was moderately overweight had been waving his hand.

"Yes, thank you," said Senator Dillon, "I think one of the main problems that the Right To Life movement and many other Americans envision with genetic engineering is the question of who will decide what genes and whose genomes will be reproduced. Will it be individual couples? If so, we may end up with twice as many boys as girls or too many athletes and not enough scientists and musicians. Or, since couples are relatively young when these reproductive decisions are made, would the next generation have a large number of individuals with the genetic constitution of the last generation's leading rock star?

"Alternatively," Senator Dillon continued, "will the federal government set quotas for the number of individuals who will be allowed to have genomes with musical talents, scientific talents, managerial talents, or even political talents?" There was a ripple of laughter from the audience.

"And who will decide which couple will be allowed children with which genetic material? Will it be by luck of the draw so that a family with musical talents might end up with children who are skilled plumbers or will musicians be required to accept children genetically engineered to be talented musicians?" Senator Dillon paused for breath and looked as though he was about to continue, but then signaled to the chair that he was finished.

"If there are no further questions of Mr. Hamilton," Senator Smathers said as he surveyed the other four senators, "Counsel will please call the next witness."

"Mr. Paul Bullock, would you please take the chair, state your name, place of residence, and affiliation?" Counsel requested.

A rather thin, intense man with a prominent nose and chin (not a perfect genetic specimen, physically at least) seated himself at the witness table and stated, "My name is Paul Bullock. I'm from Eugene, Oregon and I am president of the American Eugenics Society."

"You may give a brief opening statement if you like," said Senator Smathers.

"Thank you, Senator," replied Mr. Bullock in a carefully modulated voice. "In general terms, the American Eugenics Society supports the goal of improving the American gene pool. By this I mean improving the genetic constitution of the average American. While there are a number of approaches to achieving this goal, we do not support all of them. In the past we have mainly been interested in pursuing our goal through legislation in the areas of immigration and incentives to couples to have fewer or greater numbers of children."

"However," Mr. Bullock continued, warming to his subject, "we think that the rapidly advancing technology of human genetic engineering will make all previous approaches to eugenics obsolete and insignificant. This extraordinary technology will allow us to make improvements in the gene pool in a matter of years that either could never be accomplished by present approaches or would require many centuries. While we recognize that the science of human genetic engineering is relatively young and that much research remains to be done, we are in favor of a large federal commitment in support of this research.

"There are numerous potential benefits of an active national human genetic engineering program," he went on. "The first one which I think the vast majority of Americans can agree on is genetic engineering to eliminate genetic diseases. Examples of such diseases include sickle cell disease, hemophilia, Huntington's chorea, achondroplastic dwarfism, and many others. Elimination of these diseases would require genetic engineering of reproductive cells. Until this is accomplished, we would, of course, support genetic therapy of the somatic type as an interim measure."

Mr. Bullock paused, carefully turning one of the pages he had placed on the table in front of him, and then continued. "The second benefit we see is, in the crudest terms, improved workers. We all know that some surgeons achieve better results than others, some musicians are more gifted than others, some craftsmen are more skilled than others, some teachers are more inspiring than others, some researchers are more ingenious than others, et cetera. We believe that improvements in worker performance will result in a tremendous increase in the quality of American products. This in turn will significantly improve America's competitive position in the world economy. This same approach would be expected to improve America's defense capabilities, both through improved defense personnel and better defense equipment."

Paul Bullock looked up as if to confirm that the senators understood the significance of his last statement. Then he proceeded. "The third benefit we see is in the area of what might be called personal satisfaction. Here I am talking about individual happiness and interpersonal relationships. There is, in our opinion, a compelling body of evidence that one's genetic constitution significantly affects these areas. With genetic engineering we should be able to decrease sociopathic personality traits including tendencies toward criminality. In conclusion, while we fully recognize the difficulties in rationally instituting a national program of human genetic engineering, we feel that the potential benefits far outweigh the risks and challenges."

"Mr. Bullock," said Senator Smathers, "let me begin the questions by asking how many members there are in the American Eugenics Society?"

"Approximately sixty-five hundred," Mr. Bullock answered.

"That's a relatively small number isn't it?" asked Senator Smathers.

"Yes, but we attribute that to the current lack of effective means to pursue the goals of our society rather than a lack of public interest in those goals," Mr. Bullock responded with somewhat strained conviction.

Senator Dillon was motioning anxiously to Chairman Smathers.

"I believe the senator from South Carolina would like to continue with the questioning," Senator Smathers said.

"Thank you, Mr. Chairman," Senator Dillon began in an agitated manner. "I think Mr. Bullock is overlooking a host of practical, let alone moral, issues in his rush into science fiction. Who is going to decide which genes are propagated and how many of each genome is made? And how will it be decided which parents raise which genomes? I can't imagine the government in this role. And what if couples want to have their own natural children? I think Mr. Bullock's remarks nicely point up the terrible consequences of such a program and why the federal government should legislate against any research in human genetic engineering, with the possible exception, and I emphasize 'possible,' of gene therapy."

"Senator, if I may, I would like to clarify several points," Mr. Bullock responded, somewhat defensively. "Let me assure you that the American Eugenics Society does not underestimate the difficulties of the questions you raise. In addition, at this time we are not advocating the institution of a specific program. We are only advocating federal support for research in this area. We feel that if the United States does not develop the technology of human genetic engineering, other technologically advanced countries, such as Russia, Japan, Israel, and many of the countries of Western Europe, will. We feel that it would be dangerous for this country to fall behind in this area both from an economic and defense point of view.

"In addition," Mr. Bullock continued, having regained his composure, "there would be the problem of illegal genetically engineered offspring. By that I mean couples would illegally have genetically engineered offspring by going to legal clinics abroad, if they could afford it, or by using illegal underground clinics in this country. The situation would be similar to abortions."

"While I see your point, Mr. Bullock," responded Senator Dillon, "I don't think we want to decide such fundamental issues on the basis of convenience or whether there will be some individuals, as always, who will attempt to circumvent the law."

"I believe Senator Wong of Hawaii has a question?" Senator Smathers asked when it appeared that Senator Dillon was through.

"Yes, thank you Senator Smathers," said Senator Wong, a serious-looking, middle-aged man. "I would like to ask Mr. Bullock what his society's goals are for the American gene pool. In other words, what traits would he like to see increase in frequency and what traits would he like to see decrease in frequency?"

"We would, of course, like to see the elimination of genetic diseases," Mr. Bullock answered. "Also, in general terms, we would like to see an increase in intelligence and in other talents such as music and the other arts. In addition, as those genes that promote happiness, a pleasant personality, et cetera, are discovered, we would want to increase their frequency."

"What physical traits would you promote?" Senator Wong persisted.

"That is a difficult area," Mr. Bullock answered slowly. It was obvious he had thought about this question before. "I think most people would prefer beauty rather than ugliness in their children. But beauty is in the eye of the beholder. Presumably members of the various races and ethnic groups will want to perpetuate the best physical traits of their own groups, but that may not be the case. Never before have they had a choice. Maybe blacks will want their children to look like Swedes; maybe Jews will want children who look Japanese. More likely, there will be a variety of preferences within all racial and ethnic groups. But there will always be chauvinistic tendencies toward the best physical traits in each group."

When Senator Wong finished this line of questioning without producing anything really inflammatory, he signaled to Senator Smathers that he would relinquish the rest of his time. Senator Smathers motioned to counsel to call the next witness.

"Would Dr. Clinton Obermeyer take the witness chair?" Counsel requested. Dr. Obermeyer was a thin, thoughtful-appearing man, who wore glasses and was dressed rather plainly. After Dr. Obermeyer was seated, Counsel continued, "Please state your name, residence, and occupation."

"My name is Clinton Obermeyer. I reside in Bethesda, Maryland where I am the director of the Molecular Genetics Lab of the Institute of Reproductive Medicine at the NIH," he stated. Clinton Obermeyer, an MD, PhD, was an international authority on human genetic engineering. His research at the NIH had resulted in several important genetic techniques. One of these techniques was capable of localizing genes for specific traits on human chromosomes and another could change those genes in a specified fashion enzymatically.

"Do you have an opening statement, Dr. Obermeyer?" asked Senator Smathers.

"Yes, I have a brief statement, Senator," Dr. Obermeyer replied. "Traditionally, researchers in biomedicine have been interested in expanding our knowledge of human biology and disease on all levels because we knew that it was only through this knowledge that new treatments and cures for disease would be found. Over the past fifty years this country has supported a biomedical research program that is unprecedented in its size and in its quality. As predicted, this research program has led to numerous breakthroughs in the treatment of disease and, in some cases, to cures. We in the scientific community feel strongly that these research efforts should be continued and that these efforts will continue to improve medical care for the people of this country.

"However," Dr. Obermeyer continued, "we realize that the techniques of molecular genetics, which are now being developed, have social and political implications that legitimately extend beyond the realm of biomedical research or medical practice. These genetic techniques, while not fully developed or perfected at this time, clearly hold the potential to change the genetic constitution of individuals and entire populations. While most of us would have little reservation about correcting a defective gene that coded for hemophilia in the reproductive cells of a woman who was a carrier and wanted children, where do we draw the line?

"Would we do the same for short parents who did not want their children to grow up with the psychological burden of being exceptionally short? These children are now treated in some clinics with growth hormone which is expensive, requires repeated intramuscular injections, and carries some risks. Or would we refuse couples with below-average intelligence who wanted to give their children above-average intelligence, assuming that it could be done safely? The list of such questions is clearly endless. And these clinical situations fall far short of the difficult issues raised by cloning. What if a musical couple wanted to have a child using Itzhak Perlman's genome and he consented; is that qualitatively or morally different from donating sperm or a fertilized ovum?

"Let me conclude by saying that those of us who work in the biomedical sciences do not pretend to have the answers to these unprecedented and very fundamental moral, ethical, and social questions. However, I think I speak for the vast majority of my colleagues in saying that we do feel that research in these areas should continue. There are many potential benefits of great significance as well as risks, both known and unknown. And if we in the United States do not pursue research in these areas, it will certainly be done by others. Open public debates, such as this one, are necessary to educate and inform the general public so that rational policies on the national level can be adopted. This committee is to be commended for undertaking this hearing."

"Senator Hardiway, I believe you would like to start the questioning?" Senator Smathers inquired.

"Yes, thank you, Mr. Chairman," Senator Hardiway began. "Dr. Obermeyer, let me start by thanking you for agreeing to testify. Your expertise will be very helpful to the committee's deliberations. My first question relates to experimental or new genes. In your opening statement you referred to correcting defective genes and to cloning. In the case of correcting defective genes I presume we would know what chemical structure the gene should have normally and make the appropriate change. In the case of cloning we would know how the genome or genetic material would express itself, within limits, because we would know the original individual. In your opening statement you did not refer to a third possible approach to genetic engineering, that of changing a gene without knowing how the new gene would express itself. Could you comment on this possibility?"

"I guess I neglected to mention that possibility because I was focusing more on the positive side," Dr. Obermeyer replied with a serious expression. "During the tens of thousands of years that man has existed as a species, uncountable random mutations have occurred in human genes as experiments of nature. We know that the vast majority of these chance mutations are harmful and are either lethal or disadvantageous to the unfortunate individual who carries the mutant gene. For the foreseeable future we will not be able to predict the effect of an engineered change to a gene that results in a chemical sequence that has not been previously observed naturally. Since the results would be deleterious in almost all cases, I don't see how such genetic experimentation of this type could be justified in humans."

Senator Hardiway appeared satisfied. Senator Smathers then nodded to Senator Allesio of Massachusetts.

"Dr. Obermeyer, I must confess that genetic engineering in humans, or anything else, seems like pure science fiction to me," said Senator Allesio, a handsome man with Mediterranean looks to match his name. "Can you tell us how likely it is that genetic engineering will become technically feasible and when that time is likely to come?"

"Senator, I think even those of us who are involved in this research share your feelings about genetic engineering," replied Dr. Obermeyer. "Although 'good breeding' has always fascinated man, the current technological possibilities were completely unforeseen until relatively recently. But now, techniques are already available for limited forms of genetic engineering in man and I think most researchers in this field would agree that the techniques for making controlled changes in specific genes as well as cloning will be developed within the decade."

"Doctor, what do you see as the dangers in genetic engineering?" Senator Allesio asked.

"From a theoretical point of view I think the dangers fall into three categories," replied Dr. Obermeyer. "First, as in any aspect of medicine, there is always a chance that the intended result of a genetic treatment will not be obtained in a given individual. For example, if one or both parents carried genes predisposing their offspring to some serious disease such as diabetes, it might be desirable to change or correct those genes in the fertilized egg. The procedure to change these genes in the fertilized egg of a couple might, by accident, result in a gene with worse consequences than diabetes.

"Second," Dr. Obermeyer continued, "there is the possibility of undesirable and unforeseen results in the general population as opposed to the individual. An example might be a decrease in diversity of individual immune systems so that infections could spread more easily than is currently possible. Let me explain.

"Currently, every individual, except identical twins, has a unique genetic makeup. This means that everyone's immune system, the system that fights infections, is also somewhat different from individual to individual. This immune diversity means that not everyone is equally susceptible to a given infectious agent. Thus, in an outbreak of a new infectious agent such as a new strain of influenza, some people are less likely to contract it than others. This diversity in susceptibility provides a certain amount of enhanced survivability to the human species as a whole. If cloning of a limited number of desirable genomes should become widespread, then a significant and perhaps dangerous decrease in the ability of the population to survive some infections might occur.

"Third," Dr. Obermeyer said, slowing his delivery somewhat, "there is the theoretical possibility of deliberate misuse of this technology. I don't think examples in this category are needed."

Senator Allesio yielded the balance of his time.

"Senator Dillon, I believe you have a question," said Senator Smathers.

"Yes, thank you Senator Smathers," replied Senator Dillon. After a short pause, he peered over his reading glasses and asked, "Dr. Obermeyer would you agree that there are similarities between the technology of genetic engineering and the technology of atomic energy? The similarities that I have in mind are that both are truly revolutionary on any historic scale and that both carry the potential for great good as well as great evil."

"Senator, that analogy has been made before," Dr. Obermeyer replied with obvious discomfort. "And while I'm not fond of it, I must admit that there is some truth in the comparison. However, I think the potential for good is greater and, hopefully, the potential for evil is less."

"Why can't we pursue medical cures without genetic engineering?" Senator Dillon asked, obviously exasperated.

"The problem is that genetic diseases are extremely difficult to cure or even treat in comparison with say infections or trauma," answered Dr. Obermeyer. "Trauma and many infections can be thought of as external insults. Once the process has been stopped and the damage repaired, the individual's biological processes again function normally. With a genetic disease, the malfunction is built in and usually cannot be corrected, or even compensated for, by external therapy. An analogy would be a car with faulty spark plugs; changing the gas or driving on a different road doesn't solve the problem. Once the technology for repairing the defective gene is available, that will clearly be the most effective, least expensive, therapy."

"Senator Allesio, you have a question?" Senator Smathers asked.

"Yes, thank you," Senator Allesio replied. "Dr. Obermeyer, do you think that the problems raised by genetic engineering are best handled by legislation?"

"Well, it's my policy never to recommend more rules," Dr. Obermeyer responded with a smile and then more seriously, "but in this case, I think that the consequences are so fundamental and so far-reaching for society as a whole that legislation will be clearly needed. Probably to set up some sort of ongoing agency, perhaps like the FDA or maybe within the NIH, to review emerging technology against legislative guidelines."

"Thank you, Dr. Obermeyer," Senator Smathers interjected. "Our scheduled time has elapsed so I think we will adjourn for the day."

The broadcast returned to the studio and to Phil Brubaker, Milly Doland and Dr. Levitt.

"Milly, do you think there were any surprises from a political perspective?" asked Phil Brubaker.

"Not really, Phil," Ms. Doland replied. "As you saw Senator Dillon is a southern conservative who is against radical change in the social order in general and very suspicious of this sort of technology in particular. On the other hand, Senator Hardiway is generally supportive of new technology and I think you saw that tendency today. However, I think it is clear that the debate on genetic engineering in humans is just beginning and that the politicians are just feeling their way at this point. They, like the general public, are just beginning to understand the potential of this new technology."

"Dr. Levitt, would you comment on Dr. Obermeyer's summary of the risks of human genetic engineering?" Phil Brubaker asked.

"Yes," Dr. Levitt replied. "In general, I agree with Dr. Obermeyer. We have known each other for a long time and have collaborated on research projects in the past. I agree that one of the greatest problems is the possibility of a deleterious decrease in the diversity of the gene pool. This is only likely to happen if cloning is widely practiced. And once the current level of diversity is lost, it would be difficult to return to the original level of diversity quickly."

"Could you elaborate on the third potential hazard Dr. Obermeyer mentioned, the purposeful misuse of this technology?" Brubaker interjected.

"Well, it is conceivable that some group, most likely outside of this country, might use this technology to create individuals who physically or intellectually could be used for criminal or military purposes," Dr. Levitt replied.

"Do you think that is likely?" Brubaker asked.

"The technology is sufficiently difficult that for the time being only countries with advanced biomedical and scientific establishment could attempt such an application," Dr. Levitt answered. "In addition, since the maturation time of a human is approximately twenty years, it would require that long to produce mature genetically engineered humans."

"What countries would meet your criterion of having an advanced biomedical research establishment?" Brubaker inquired.

"Roughly, the list would include Sweden, England, Germany, France, Israel, Russia, Japan, and the United States at this time," replied Dr. Levitt.

"Did it surprise you that Dr. Obermeyer recommended legislation?" Brubaker asked.

"Not at all," Dr. Levitt responded. "I don't expect the government to interfere in the strictly medical or technical aspects, but I think government, as the only collective decision-making body we have, is the appropriate institution to determine which genetically engineered genomes can legally be used and how it will be decided who gets them.

Without some degree of central planning, it would be possible that genomes would be used that carry significant abnormalities or that there would be an undesirable distribution of genomes. For instance, if half of all couples opted for genomes that produced outstanding musicians, we would have a surplus of musicians and a shortage of other skills."

"I don't see how government can make these very personal decisions for individual in an acceptable way," remarked Brubaker.

"Frankly, I don't either, but I don't see any workable alternative either," replied Dr. Levitt with a smile that seemed somewhat inappropriate.

"You're going to miss the turn!" Anne yelled.

I quickly maneuvered into the right-hand lane and exited the interstate.

"What were you daydreaming about this time?" Anne chided.

"I was envisioning what televised senate hearings on genetic engineering might be like," I explained somewhat embarrassed. "You can imagine all the prejudices and fears those hearings are going to elicit."

"Yeah, I'm sure you'll be glued to the TV when they happen," Anne replied knowingly.

6

The Reproductive Clinc

Åfter two days of looking we found a great apartment in an older section of Bethesda, only three blocks from the NIH. Although Washington, DC is clearly a metropolis, it seemed refreshingly small and uncrowded compared to New York.

Now we both had two weeks before starting our new jobs, perfect for exploring the history and institutions of the capital, and unwinding from six years of academic grind in Manhattan.

Most of my security clearance for working at the Brookings Institution had been handled before I left New York. It was relatively low key. The FBI had talked to friends in my hometown as well as to acquaintances in New York. They also had investigated Anne's past. Almost embarrassingly, they found nothing of interest in either case.

The Brookings Institution is basically a think tank. The thinking is done by a group of overly educated, slightly weird, academic types and the tank is a group of buildings with the look of a small college campus. Various institutions and agencies, mostly belonging to the federal government, commission analyses of various national or world problems, or of possible future problems.

I thought I might be assigned to work on something like germ warfare, but it was actually more interesting than that. I wasn't supposed to talk to anyone about it, but somehow it seemed OK to talk to Anne about it, or at least very awkward not to. I've always thought that, in a job like this, whether you discuss secrets with your wife probably separates the hardcore operatives from those who more or less find themselves in the job.

One warm summer evening when, at Anne's request, we were walking through the National Art Gallery, I began thinking about what the future clinics for reproductive genetics might be like. There were already physicians who specialized in medical genetics. They spent their time counseling families with known genetic diseases, telling them the probability that the disease in question would be passed on to their male or female offspring. But at present there was no preventive genetic therapy, only amniocentesis for diagnosis and elective abortion, and preimplantation diagnosis and selection in conjunction with in vitro fertilization.

"Good morning, Susan," I said as I arrived at the clinic office. I pictured myself working in the reproductive genetics clinic in the outpatient building back at Cornell and the New York Hospital, "What's on the schedule this morning?"

"There are almost all new patients today," she replied. That meant longer sessions for explaining the intricacies of having a genetically engineered child. Susan ushered in Tom and Marcie Johnston, a reasonably attractive couple, probably in their late twenties.

"Good morning," I said. "I understand that you are interested in having a genetically engineered child for your next baby."

"Yes, Dr. Kenton, at least we would like to consider it," Marcie replied.

I looked at the questionnaire they had filled out with Susan's help: name, address, age, and reproductive history. The last being number of pregnancies and outcomes: live birth, stillbirth (dead infant at term), spontaneous abortion (medical term for miscarriage), or elective abortion (medical term for induced or therapeutic abortion). Marcie had had three pregnancies: two live births and one intervening spontaneous abortion in the first trimester.

"How did you hear about this program?" I asked.

"We read about it in several magazines and heard about it on TV," Marcie answered. "But mainly we have a friend who has done it."

"How old is your friend's child?" I inquired.

"He's almost two now," Marcie responded.

"How is he doing so far?" I continued.

"He's doing just fine. He seems very bright and he's a delight to be around," Marcie commented.

"And he's certainly better looking than his parents," Tom Johnston added. We all smiled.

"This program is still experimental and regulated by rules set up by the NIH," I explained. "You must have at least one natural child surviving to be eligible to participate in the program. In addition, you must agree to participate in periodic follow-ups. These will entail interviews of the parents and the child and, after a certain age, psychological testing of the child. In addition, each couple is allowed to have only one child by this program."

"We have no problem with those requirements," said Marcie. "What can we know about the donors of the genes?"

"Let me answer that question by first explaining some of the general philosophy of the program," I went on. "As you probably know, the program is a method of improving the so called 'gene pool.' By that I mean the average quality of genes in the population at large. Currently, everyone carries a certain number of good genes, a few bad or deleterious genes, and a large number of average genes. In addition, each parent gives only half of his or her genes to each child and chance determines which half.

"Thus, until now, the only control one had over the genes he or she gave to his or her children was in the selection of a mate," I continued. "Until recently we had no way to select the genes of our children in a controlled fashion.

"In this program," I went on, "individuals who have been successful in life, who are healthy, who have a pleasant or at least reasonable personality, and who are reasonably attractive physically are invited to be donors. If they agree, they receive a complete medical evaluation for any signs of genetic disease or abnormalities including an analysis of their chromosomes – chromosomes are the structures within cells that carry our genes. Then blood cells containing their genes are crossed at least once with another selected donor to produce a new unique genome or set of genes. Thus, there is no cloning."

"So they never use one set of genes more than once, is that right?" asked Tom.

"That is correct," I answered. "But they do keep some cells with the same new genome for research purposes. Analysis of the genes can be correlated with follow-up data from the child, who was produced with that genome."

"But you still don't control whether the new set of genes includes only the best genes of the donors or the worst or the average ones?" Tom questioned.

"Unfortunately, that's correct," I agreed. "Selecting the best genes is not technically possible at this time. The effort is directed toward taking genes from genomes that have produced superior individuals, if you will. The method does not guarantee that the new set of genes will produce individuals with traits that are as desirable as those of the donors. However, because there are so many genes in the human genome, more than twenty thousand, it is unlikely that a cross between two genomes would result in all bad genes. But, by the same token, the cross is unlikely to result in a genome consisting of all the best genes of the donors as well."

"It all sounds very clinical and unnatural," Marcie interjected half smiling. "I do get to carry the baby, don't I?"

"Yes, no artificial gestation," I responded, trying to reassure her. "You gestate or incubate the baby, deliver the baby, and raise the child. The only difference is that you don't conceive the child."

"How do the genes get into the womb?" Marcie asked with a blush as if it was something she should know.

"Good question," I replied. "First we obtain one of your own eggs from your ovary. This is done with a long tube, using ultrasound guidance; I'll explain the procedure in detail later. The nucleus of the egg which contains your genes, actually half of them, is removed using a very small needle. The new genes in their own nucleus are then inserted into your egg. Your egg with its new genetic blueprint is incubated outside your body for a few days and then placed in your uterus. The egg doesn't always implant and start to develop, so the procedure may need to be repeated. The chance of implantation on any one try is about fifty percent."

"Tell me how you get one of my eggs," Marcie asked apprehensively.

"Well, this is going to sound worse than it is," I replied. "Each egg develops inside a little fluid-filled sac on the surface of the ovary. Using ultrasound imaging we can locate where the egg is on the ovary. The best way to do the ultrasound imaging is with the bladder distended, so we have you drink a lot of water just before we do the procedure. Then we take a long thin tube and place it in the bladder through the urethra, the natural opening in the bladder. This may result in some discomfort, but not pain. Using the ultrasound images we guide the tube toward the ovary which lies just outside of the bladder wall. When everything is lined up just right, a needle within the tube is pushed through the bladder wall into the cyst containing the egg, and the egg is aspirated into the needle. The needle is then withdrawn. Since the bladder is relatively insensitive to pain, no anesthesia is needed.

"That definitely sounds unnatural," Marcie said with a laugh.

"To change the subject a bit," Tom said, "what are the legalities of this type of reproduction? I assume the donors have no legal rights to the child."

"That's correct," I responded. "Each donor signs an agreement that he or she relinquishes all claim to the offspring and will make no effort to determine what couple or couples receive some of his or her genes."

"And as I understand it, we have no choice whether we get a boy or a girl, or whether the donor's talents are scientific, artistic, or whatever?" Tom asked.

"That's true," I answered. "The idea is to keep the sex ratio at one to one and for the parents to have no preconceived notions as to how the child should be raised. However, you do get to choose the race of the child: Caucasian, Asian, or Negro."

"We would want a Caucasian child," Marcie said.

"That's fine," I said.

"Who decides which individuals will be donors and which genes will be sent to which couple?" Tom asked.

"The selection of donors is made by a committee at the NIH," I explained. "The committee is composed of physicians, clergy, and ethicists, similar to the ethics committees in hospitals. The selection of a genome for a particular couple is made randomly. In other words there is no attempt made to match the talents and tastes of the prospective parents with those of the genes' donors. In general, the process is somewhat similar to the procedures used by sperm banks to obtain and distribute sperm, except that the technical aspects are much more complicated."

"It seems like it might be better to try and match talents and tastes, as you say, rather than doing it by chance," Tom commented.

"I don't necessarily disagree with that," I replied. "But with the current approach the requested talents couldn't be guaranteed. Also, I think the feeling is that society is not yet ready for made-to-order babies. Healthy, talented ones, maybe. But not ones with specified parts like the Mr. Potato Head game."

"What do we do next?" Marcie asked.

"Next we would like you to go home, think about what we've discussed today, and read some pamphlets that review the details of the process," I said. "Then, if you're ready to proceed, we'll see you back in two weeks and make the necessary arrangements. This will include an interview by a social worker with both of you at home."

"That sounds fine," Marcie said. "Thank you, Dr. Kenton."

I saw the Johnstons to the office door. Their interview had taken thirty minutes, which meant the next couple would be waiting.

Susan motioned a black couple my way.

"This is Jim and Rhoda Harrington. This is Dr. Kenton," she said handing me the usual paperwork.

"Come in," I said, closing the door behind them. "Have a seat."

"Thank you," Jim said.

"You're interested in our program of having children using donor genes?" I asked, resisting the temptation to call them designer genes.

"Yes," Rhoda replied. "We were referred by Dr. Goldfarb."

"I see that you both have sickle cell trait," I said as I looked at their chart. Dr. Goldfarb was a hematologist at New York Hospital.

"Yes, and we've decided not to have any of our own children because of the risk of sickle cell disease," Rhoda responded.

The situation was that both Rhoda and Jim carried one gene for hemoglobin S (the sickle cell gene) and one gene for hemoglobin A (the normal hemoglobin gene). The result is that half of the hemoglobin in each of their red blood cells is of the abnormal S type and the other half is normal; neither gene is dominant. This condition is usually asymptomatic. However, one-fourth of their children would be expected to have two S genes (one from each parent) which would result in sickle cell disease or anemia; this condition causes significant morbidity and often death in childhood. An additional half of their children would be carriers like their parents and the remaining fourth would be normal.

"As Dr. Goldfarb may have told you," I said, "in general a couple is required to have had at least one child naturally before they can be considered for this program. However, an exception is made for couples who do not have children because of the risk of genetic disease."

"Yes, we've discussed this at length with Dr. Goldfarb," Jim said. "While we realize that twenty-five percent of our children would be normal and another fifty percent would be asymptomatic although carriers, we would prefer not to take the risk. We both have had family members who died of sickle cell disease; we feel it would be unfair to the affected child as well as the rest of the family."

"That's not to say that it wasn't a difficult decision," Rhoda added.

"I'm sure it wasn't an easy decision," I said. "But I can understand your feelings."

I went on to explain the philosophy of the program; the requirement of an interview with a social worker in their home; the technical aspects of harvesting the ovum, exchanging genetic material in the ovum, and transferring it back to Rhoda's uterus; and the fact that they would have no choice in the sex of the child or the type of talents of the donors although they could chose the race of the child.

"We understand," said Jim. "In fact we've given a lot of thought to the selection of race. And our feeling is that we want a Caucasian child."

I tried not to look surprised – doctors are supposed to always maintain equanimity and, of course, this possibility had been foreseen, but this was the first time one of my couples had wanted a child of a different race.

"Why do you want a Caucasian child?" I asked matter-of-factly.

"Quite simply, because of the pervasive discrimination against blacks in this country," Jim replied. "We don't question that this is a great country and that discrimination against minorities may be less here than in many places, but, nonetheless, it's a terrible cross to bear."

"If we were living in a predominantly black country, we would feel differently," Rhoda added.

"I understand," I said. It was clear that they had already given this decision much thought. Although I probably should have discussed with them the possible problems of society's attitudes toward the child for completeness' sake, it didn't seem appropriate. They probably understood this far better than I did.

"It's not that we feel inferior," Jim said with a smile. Although he had not gone to college, he had a good job with a manufacturing company and had been a star athlete in high school, Rhoda also had a good job, which she was planning to give up, at least temporarily, when the baby was born (although this was not a program requirement).

With no more questions, it was agreed that they would proceed with the social worker interview and return in two weeks.

Barry and Greta Ashkenazi were next; this was their second visit.

"Please be seated," I said as Susan handed me their chart.

Barry was an attorney with one of those large Manhattan law firms and Greta was a buyer with Bloomingdales. They were an unusual couple, at least genetically, in that they were both carriers of Tay-Sachs disease, an inherited disease of abnormal ganglioside metabolism. (Ganglioside is a type of fat found in nerve cells.) Afflicted individuals appear normal at birth, but during the first year of life they manifest mental and motor deterioration which rapidly progresses to blindness, deafness, and muscle rigidity. Death from infection usually occurs by age three. There is no treatment.

Among carriers of this disease Barry and Greta were not unusual in that they were both Jews of Eastern European decent. Jews have at least a thirty times greater incidence of Tay-Sachs disease than non-Jews, and the highest incidence occurs in Jews of Polish ancestry. Greta's sister had had a child who died of Tay-Sachs and both Barry and Greta had been identified as carriers of the disease by blood tests.

While prenatal diagnosis in the second trimester of pregnancy by amniocentesis (sampling the fluid within the uterus around the developing fetus) was possible, it was not entirely reliable and, if positive, led to the emotional agonies of abortion. Alternatively, a newer procedure, preimplantation diagnosis and selection, can be used in conjunction with in vitro fertilization. Several eggs are fertilized in a petri dish. Once they reach the eight cell stage a single cell is removed and tested for the Tay-Sachs gene. Then an embryo is selected that does not have the Tay-Sachs gene for implantation in the uterus.

"We're pretty much ready to proceed," Barry said. The interview with the social worker had gone fine. "But we're wondering if there isn't some way that we can have more choice over the genes that we get. We'd like to be able to select a musician rather than a scientist, both of us are amateur musicians, and we would like to have some say as to physical appearance and personality. The NIH clearly has this information."

"That's quite understandable and a common request," I responded. "However, the NIH is concerned about several things including creation of personality or donor cults, the possibility that certain donors will become unduly popular, and that the desired variability in the program, that is in the genes, will not be maintained."

"What about the Caribbean clinics?" Barry asked. "We've heard that there are clinics on some of the Caribbean islands that are not under US jurisdiction and that they allow you to know all about the donors. The donors are successful people, genetically endowed people, who are paid for the use of their genes. In addition, you can choose the sex of the baby."

"Yes, I know about those clinics," I replied. I had suspected that this question was coming. The supermarket magazines were full of stories on these offshore clinics. "They don't publish their results so there is no detailed or scientific information on their methods, results, or complications. And we don't know how rigorously the donors are screened for genetic disease or behavioral abnormalities. However, it is certainly not illegal to use them. As you probably know," I said looking at Barry, "Western law has always been very reluctant to intrude into the area of procreation."

"We have a friend who knows someone in Dallas who got pregnant at one of those clinics," Greta said, somewhat excitedly. "They were able to select the two donors from over a hundred possibilities. And so far their baby has turned out just perfect."

"How much information were they given about the donors?" I asked.

"From what we understand, they were given complete biographical sketches, but were not given the donor's names or addresses or any way to identify the individuals," Barry answered. "There is one disadvantage, however. The cost is about three times as much."

"I wish there were some way for us to be more certain about the quality of the Caribbean clinics," Greta added.

"I'm afraid that I can't help you with that," I said. "I just don't have that information."

The Ashkenazis decided to postpone going ahead, at least with our clinic. I felt pretty sure that the lure of being able to select the donor genes and thus the looks, talents, and personality of their offspring would be decisive.

Anne had steered us into the Western Art section of the gallery and was busy admiring a large Remington.

"I think it's definitely going to happen," I said.

"Never, people will want their own kids," Anne replied, she usually knew where my thoughts had been. "Anyway the whole idea of clones is somehow repulsive," she added. "It's worse than marrying your brother."

"Yes, but less genetic risk," I quipped. "But I'm thinking of the couple who are carriers for some genetic disease. Giving them a child using selected donor genes seems a lot better than adoption, and, anyway, there's a shortage of kids for adoption."

"Why not just harvest several eggs from the woman, fertilize them, determine which fertilized eggs have the defective gene and which don't, and then transfer a good one into the uterus?" Anne asked casually as we moved on to the next gallery.

The procedure that Anne was referring to was a very promising relatively recent development, but I could tell Anne really wasn't in the mood to discuss this topic so I changed the subject. Why ruin a potentially great evening?

7

Transition Generation –
United States

I was just beginning to feel comfortable in my job at the Brookings Institution when Dr. Gardiner, the head of the molecular biology section, asked to see me in his office.

"Bryan, there's an urgent need for an expert in molecular genetics at the Pentagon," Dr. Gardiner began. "I know you've only been here about six months, but this is top priority from a national security point of view."

"At the Pentagon?" I asked with surprise. I didn't usually think of the Pentagon as a bastion of science, especially not molecular genetics.

"They need someone with both medical and scientific training," Dr. Gardiner explained. "I don't know what the need is – it's classified. But we have a contract to supply the Pentagon with consultants. I don't anticipate this assignment lasting more than a year," he added.

Somehow, just at that moment, the clause in my contract about accepting temporary assignments (up to twelve months) at other locations surfaced in my consciousness.

"Let me think about it overnight," I said. "Will I be officed here or at the Pentagon?"

"At the Pentagon," Dr. Gardiner replied with a smile. "You won't be in the military though; you'll be a consultant at the very highest level. It'll look good on your CV and you'll be serving your country at the same time." I've noticed that all good administrators are adept at flattery.

Well, Anne wasn't exactly ecstatic. She hadn't been delighted with my decision to leave academic medicine, even if only temporarily. Unstated, most of the time, was her conviction that any other job was intellectually inferior. I didn't really disagree.

That night over dinner we fantasized what it would be like working at the Pentagon. Would I learn any deep, dark secrets? Would I learn what the Russian military is really like?

"You might look pretty good in a uniform, particularly a navy uniform," Anne commented.

"I'll just be a civilian consultant. It has more status," I answered defensively.

"Too bad, there's something sexy about a man in uniform," Anne teased.

After dinner Anne worked on a manuscript she was preparing for publication while I did the dishes. The deal was she fixed dinner and I cleaned up. One advantage of washing dishes was that it could be done by rote, leaving time for thinking.

Again, I found myself thinking about the future impact of genetic engineering, trying to imagine what it would be like during the "transition generation." That is, the generation when most older members of society would have natural genomes ("wild type" would be the biological phrase) and most younger members would have genetically engineered genomes.

I imagined that Anne and I were once again back on staff at Cornell and New York Hospital, we were both doing clinical genetics, and we had two genetically engineered children; we had also had one of our own. I was working in the Reproductive Genetics Clinic as before, helping couples have genetically engineered "offspring." (Offspring maybe wasn't quite the right word anymore.) Anne was in the Division of Clinical Genetics in the Department of Pediatrics. Although there were now many fewer children born with genetic diseases, her division was busier than ever evaluating the results of the National Program for Genetic Improvement, the NPGI.

The NIH research projects that were designed to demonstrate the feasibility of genetic engineering in humans had clearly been a success. Using the woman's ovum and substituting a nucleus containing a genome from two donors, a 55 percent pregnancy rate had been achieved. That rate is even better than the natural rate. That is, with unprotected intercourse the average couple has only a 25 percent chance of becoming pregnant each month.

The higher pregnancy rate probably relates to the fact that almost half of natural conceptions abort during the first trimester of pregnancy and a large proportion of these are found to have genetic abnormalities. In fact, these miscarriages are the primary mechanism of natural selection. In genetically engineered embryos, essentially all genetic abnormalities are eliminated.

The genetically engineered offspring were also very successful. In the aggregate, they were clearly more successful than the "natural" or "wild" population. In some families with relatively limited genetic abilities, the genetically engineered offspring clearly stood out. While examples of this situation were not new, its frequency of occurrence certainly was.

However, the genetically engineered offspring were not as successful as the donors of their genomes. This could be explained without resorting to the possibility that the genetically engineered offspring had a less advantageous environment than the environment enjoyed by the donors.

The explanation, instead, most likely lay in the genetic principle of "regression to the mean." Simply stated, this meant that a couple at one extreme of the genetic spectrum for a given multifactorial trait (that is a trait determined by more than one gene such as height, intelligence, lack of intelligence, and so on) will have children who are closer to the average or mean for that trait than they were.

It is somewhat like forming a new football team from two existing outstanding teams. The first string can be thought of as the dominant genes, the ones that are expressed and the ones that primarily determine the team's record. The second string players are the recessive genes. If you form the new team by randomly picking half the members of each team (as is done in "picking" the genes of offspring in natural reproduction), you could end up with many second string players or a team with great depth in offense, but no defense. By chance it is be difficult to pick a balanced team with at least one good player at each position.

Of course cloning would avoid the problem of regression to the mean; you would know exactly what you were getting, sort of like a McDonald's hamburger or perhaps a Rolls Royce. But there would be no room for trying new combinations, albeit in the case of natural reproduction the combinations are selected by chance. And there would be the risks that accompany lack of diversity.

That afternoon Anne was giving the weekly Friday afternoon pediatric department seminar. I was planning to attend since the topic, "Current Status of Genetic Engineering in Humans: Fifteen Years of the NPGI" was in my field. Also, I enjoyed Anne's performances. They were always well done, particularly for someone with a natural genome, as I was fond of telling her.

The conference room in the pediatric wing of the New York Hospital was packed with pediatric residents, pediatric faculty, and various other interested parties. Genetic engineering was a much hotter topic than say "Inflammatory Bowel Disease" or "The Differential Diagnosis of Dementia." I have noticed that on these occasions Anne's attire is always a little more seductive and perhaps less professional than usual. The sweater is a little tighter, the skirt a little shorter. She wouldn't admit it, but she probably feels it gives her a bit more leverage over her audience, at least the male members. And I really wouldn't want to tamper with the genes that code for this behavior.

"In this two-part seminar," Anne began, "I'm going to review the status and progress of the NPGI in the United States; then in the second part next week, I'll review the progress of genetic engineering in the rest of the world. Most of the statistics that I'll show today come from the most recent annual report of the National Program for Genetic Improvement.

"In the United States last year, just over half, fifty four percent, of infants were products of genetic engineering," Anne said, pointing to the table in the first slide. "Participation is voluntary although there are, of course, tax incentives. The NPGI, through its regional committees, now has over one million well screened donors. This number is just below the goal of five percent of the population.

"As you know," Anne continued, "the donor program as well as the recipient program is voluntary so that very talented individuals can choose not to participate. However, NPGI regularly solicits donors by advertising."

The advertising, such as "If you think you possess unusual talents, you should contact your local NPGI office. There's no better way to insure your country's future!" were controversial and provided material for endless jokes.

"The program is also confidential," Anne added. "The NPGI records are not open to the public – similar to the IRS. But in addition, the donors are never told whether their genome has been used and if so with what frequency."

"What does the screening process consist of?" asked a physician from India who was doing a fellowship in the pediatric department. Most of the other attendees knew from personal experience what the screening procedure consisted of.

"The screening process involves a thorough medical evaluation plus sequencing of the potential donor's entire genome," Anne responded. "If any genes on the 'unwanted' list are found, the donor is not used. All deleterious recessive genes are not eliminated since, at this time, that would make the program too restrictive; it would be hard to find enough donors. And as long as you know that a given donor has the undesirable recessive gene in his genome, you can be sure that his genome is never crossed with another donor with the same deleterious recessive gene. At this time no attempt is made to correct the defective gene although this is, of course, done in genetic engineering in animals and this approach in man is currently being considered by the NIH.

"The 'soft' part of the screening procedure," Anne went on, "is the evaluation of talents: the individual's scientific, artistic, business, and/or political talents. And even softer is the evaluation of behavioral traits, personality, and physical appearance. This area has been a boon to the job market for psychologists!"

"How is physical appearance evaluated?" asked one resident. "Is it evaluated by members of the opposite sex or the same sex?" The question, predictably, elicited a round of laughter.

"It's evaluated by a bisexual committee, of course," Anne promptly replied with a smile. "The final selection is done by a NPGI committee based on all of the data including the results of standard interviews although the committee itself does not interview the prospective donor."

"How detailed are the provisions in the law setting up the NPGI?" asked one of the residents. "I mean how much leeway does the selection committee have?"

"Currently, the selection committee has a great deal of discretion, although there are always those in Congress pushing their own pet traits or genes," Anne responded going on to the next slide. "As you can see here the law does specify an equal sex distribution and category percentages for men and women. For men its fifty percent percent businessmen, thirty percent scientists/engineers, ten percent artist, and ten percent leaders/lawyers/politicians. For women its thirty-five percent homemakers, thirty percent businesswomen, twenty percent scientists/engineers, ten percent artists, and five percent leaders/lawyers/politicians."

"There's obvious male chauvinism in the last category," Anne remarked. "So far we haven't been able to identify the responsible gene. It seems to be the whole Y chromosome. It doesn't code for anything else!"

Anne's sarcasm related to the fact that only males carry the Y chromosome (or perhaps, more accurately those who carry the Y chromosome are males). The Y chromosome is by far the smallest of the forty-six chromosomes in the human genome, and its function and mechanism of action are not well understood.

"It looks like there could be a lot of overlap between categories," one of the pediatric faculty commented.

"True," Anne answered. "An engineer in a middle level executive position with AT&T who was an excellent pianist could qualify under business, scientist/engineer, and artist. Again, this gives the selection committees a lot of flexibility."

"This next slide shows the makeup of the Central NPGI Committee," Anne said as she tried to push the pace a bit. "There are two representatives from each category plus two ethicists, usually a theologian or academician, and the director of the NIH, ex officio. All are appointed by the president with confirmation by the Senate and they all serve staggered four-year terms except, of course, the NIH director. The Central NPGI Committee, based at NIH, does not select any of the individuals itself, but it sets policy and formulates detailed guidelines for the one hundred regional selection committees. Most, but not all, of these Committees are based at medical schools.

"The patient goes to her obstetrician who usually is not officed at the medical school, and the patient has one or more ova removed under ultrasound guidance," Anne continued. "The ova are frozen and sent to the NPGI regional center where a hybrid donor nucleus with a full complement of chromosomes is substituted for the natural nucleus in at least one ovum. The ovum or ova, now fertilized zygotes, are refrozen and returned to the patient's obstetrician for transfer into patient's uterus. Only one zygote is transferred at a time. When there is evidence that one zygote has successfully implanted, then no more transfers are made unless the patient aborts. If the patient delivers a normal child, the remaining zygotes are not used.

"How much information do parents get about the various donors when they are selecting a genome?" asked one of the medical students.

"I was just coming to that," Anne replied. This many interruptions were unusual, but human genetic engineering was a hot topic within medical centers as well as with the lay public.

"In general, the NPGI has tried to give rather detailed information to prospective parents in order to encourage use of the program," Anne continued. "The parents are allowed to choose the characteristics listed in this slide: race, ancestral country of origin and ethnic group, height and hair color, facial characteristics, athleticism, talent categories, and health records. The names and pictures of the donors are in the NPGI records, but are not given to the prospective parents."

"How many donor combinations are there to choose from?" asked the same medical student.

"There are many possible donor pairs for each combination of traits," Anne answered. "Therefore, when the prospective parents select a set of traits, they are not specifying a unique pair of donors.

"And the first time they are not selecting a sex," Anne went on. "The couple specifies the desired traits for both a boy and a girl and the sex is determined randomly. If the couple decides to have a second genetically engineered child, they can specify the opposite sex of the first child or, if there is a national imbalance by more than two percent they can specify the less represented sex.

"Now let me review the follow-up procedures that have been established by the NPGI and that are required of the parents," Anne continued as she went on to the next slide. "The parents notify the regional NPGI center at the time of the birth of the genetically engineered child and a social worker interviews the parents and makes sure that copies of the pregnancy and delivery records are forwarded to the NPGI office. A social worker then interviews the parents in their home annually until the child leaves home.

"The child," Anne continued, "is evaluated at the regional NPGI Center at six-month intervals for the first two years and then annually. This evaluation consists of both a physiological portion and a medical portion. These data on each child are then sent to the National NPGI Center in Rockville, Maryland where they are correlated with the gene sequence of each child. This process will eventually lead to the ability to predict the physical, mental, and behavioral characteristics which result from various genes and combinations of genes."

"How will that information be used?" asked Dr. Oldham, chairman of the pediatrics department.

"At present, it is just stored." Anne answered. "In the near future it will be used to eliminate donor combinations which result in genetic disease that was not predicted in advance. It, of course, could also be used to increase the frequency of use of donors and donor combinations which give the most favorable outcomes."

"Is it possible to splice all the best genes into an ideal genome?" one of the pediatric residents asked.

"At this time," Anne responded, "gene-splicing technology is not capable of that degree of precision. However, I think it is clear that in the not-too-distant future we will have that capability."

Without waiting for additional discussion of this point, Anne went on to her next slide.

"The NPGI program has now been underway for almost fifteen years," she stated. "The follow-up data to date shows pretty much what you'd expect. The incidence of genetic disease in the genetically engineered population is only twelve percent of the incidence in the non genetically engineered population. The remaining genetic disease is caused by genes that we did not know how to screen for in the donor genome and to a lesser extent, mutations.

"The standardized intelligence test results for the genetically engineered children are, on average, at the seventy-third percentile compared to the fiftieth percentile in non-genetically engineered children," Anne said pointing to the graph in her slide. "This is a very significant difference, but not as high as the average donor group IQ. Similar test results at similar ages are, of course, not available for this donor group, but the best available data would put the donors, on average, in about the eighty-fifth percentile. The lower results for the genetically engineered group can be explained by the 'regression to the mean' phenomenon."

Anne was referring to a well-known genetic principle. It takes just the right combination of many genes to give high intelligence. When you cross the genes from two donors with high intelligence, the resultant genome will have a lot of genes that potentially code for high intelligence, but it is likely that they will not be in the optimal combination.

Anne went on to the next slide, "This slide summarizes the trends in physical features. There has been a definite increase in the percentage of children with blond hair, from about twenty percent to forty-two percent. There has been a small increase in average height, but the main change in height has been fewer very short and very tall children. The extremes in height don't seem to be very popular. Similar changes have occurred in ear, nose, and mouth size; the trend is toward a medium size with less of the extremes. The same is true of body habitus; there is less obesity and less frailty.

"The overall sex ratio has stayed even," Anne continued as she went to the next slide. "Originally there was concern that the sex ratio might become unbalanced. Since it was decided that the first genetically engineered child for each couple would be of random sex and that the second one would be of the opposite sex, a couple could stop after the first one if it happened to be a boy, for instance, but opt for a second one if the first one was a girl knowing that the second one would then be a boy.

"However, the provisions that a couple could select the opposite sex from what they would otherwise get for the second child if this would tend to equalize the national sex ratio and that a couple could have a third genetically engineered child without an income tax penalty if they accepted the sex that would tend to equalize the national ratio have negated any tendency toward predominance of one sex. The data does show that these provisions were needed and that there was a modest tendency to prefer boys."

I was surprised that Anne resisted making any snide remarks at this point.

"This last slide shows the participation rate," Anne said coming to the end of the first seminar. "Over the fifteen years that the NPGI has been in existence the percentage of couples having one or more children through the NPGI has increased from eight percent in the first year to seventy-three percent currently. This figure will probably never reach a hundred percent as long as the program is voluntary. There will always be some couples who don't want children, want only natural children, or who end up with all they want naturally by poor planning or bad luck.

"The dramatic increase in participation," Anne went on, "is attributable to several factors. First and most importantly, the high quality of the genetically engineered children has encouraged more and more couples to participate. Second, there has been a very low complication rate from the impregnation process, only an occasional, easily treatable infection at the time of transfer. And last, but not least, there are the tax advantages.

"Currently, of the couples who participate," Anne continued, "seventy-one percent have two genetically engineered children, twenty-four percent have one, and five percent have more than two. More than two is possible because of divorce and remarriage or because of willingness to accept a third genetically engineered child of the deficient sex, deficient in quantity, not quality, of course." (The deficient sex currently was female.)

"That concludes my brief summary of the NPGI experience," Anne said. "Next week I'll summarize the experience to date outside of the United States."

"If I may, I'd like to make two comments," Dr. Oldham said as Anne finished. Department chairmen always seem to feel a need to comment at the end of a presentation. "The technology of genetic engineering is unique in that it cannot directly benefit the generation that developed it; their genes are not changed. In contrast, antibiotics, anesthesia, and vaccines have all benefitted those already living. Second, although Anne didn't mention it, the cost of the NPGI program including the small army of workers needed to gather data on the genetically engineered products, is less than the estimated savings from the reduction in genetic disease and disabilities."

At the end of the post seminar questions and discussion, Anne and I walked to the parking garage and headed home to Westchester County. Home to our two genetically engineered kids.

8

A Parent's Point of View

The nearly one-hour commute home was always a good time to discuss family affairs, particularly the children. After having made the trip hundreds of times, it no longer required much in the way of conscious effort. I inserted the car into East River Drive rush-hour traffic and turned the driving over to whatever part of the brain handles such repetitive tasks.

"Alison really did well on her test scores," Anne commented referring to our seven-year-old daughter and the aptitude test, her first, which she had just taken at school. Alison had scored in the ninety-third percentile on a nationwide basis.

"I knew she would," I added. She had learned to read almost anything by age five, she could carry on adult like conversations, and arithmetic was a breeze for her.

"No, you didn't," Anne replied knowingly.

In fact, we really hadn't been sure how she would do. We saw her as very bright, but then she was also part of the transition generation. About half the kids her age were genetically engineered, GEM kids as they were called for genetic engineering of man, and the old standards didn't apply anymore.

It was an ongoing debate exactly how to grade kids when half of them were GEM kids with almost uniformly high IQs and the other half were "natural" kids with the traditional spectrum of IQs. It had been decided that there was no good or workable alternative to using the old relative system. A new grading system in which 60 percent of the students got As, 10 percent got Bs, 10 percent got Cs, and 10 percent got Ds would simply make an A meaningless. And besides, in another generation essentially all children would be genetically engineered.

"I wonder if Bryan will do as well." I remarked. Bryan III, our other genetically engineered child, was five and not as precocious as Alison.

"Sure, boys just don't develop as fast as girls," Anne replied. But to this point Bryan had been clearly bright (by the old standards anyway), but not outstanding. And then there was no reason to expect our GEM kids to be brighter than other couples' GEM kids.

Genetic engineering of children had an unprecedented social-leveling effect. Now every couple, regardless of their own genetic endowment, could have a good chance of rearing a child with exceptional talents and an almost certainty of having a bright healthy child. Of course, this aspect of genetic engineering bothered the hell out of some who happened to be endowed with better-than-average genes before genetic engineering. While they couldn't be sure that their natural offspring would maintain the family's relative genetic advantage, the odds were certainly in their favor.

"I think genetic engineering has resulted in an increased emphasis on environmental quality for kids," I commented. "Since most families have GEM kids with similar genes, families now compete environmentally. No longer can the upper class depend on superior genes."

"People feel that if their kids don't do well, they can't blame it on the genes, it must be a result of the upbringing," Anne added simplifying a bit. Many families had one or more natural children although the trend was definitely toward more and more genetically engineered children. GEM kids and natural kids in the same family generated a variety of psychological problems. Some of these problems were well known from families with adopted and natural children. But some aspects were new.

On the plus side, most families had GEM kids and were, therefore, not the minority as was the case with families with adopted children. On the other side, the GEM kids, in general, were smarter than the natural kids. Thus, many parents had to contend with the feelings that result from having GEM kids who are smarter than their own natural children.

Unfortunately, Anne and I weren't faced with that potential problem. We had decided to have our first child naturally. Bryan Jr. was born with cystic fibrosis; and died at the age of three years and two months. (That's why our GEM son is Bryan III.) Cystic fibrosis is a genetic disease of the recessive type, which means that both Anne and I are carriers and that we both passed one of the defective genes on to our son. Although the disease is not well understood, the most serious clinical manifestation is usually pulmonary insufficiency secondary to abnormal mucous production by the lungs and recurrent pneumonias. Cystic fibrosis gradually, but relentlessly, debilitates and weakens its victim. And when the lung infections flare up, intravenous antibiotics and hospitalization are required.

That's the clinical description. From a parent's point of view it's a nightmare from which you never wake up. We were lucky in that Bryan Jr. could be treated at home since Anne was a pediatrician. (Anne gave up her job during the time Bryan Jr. was with us.) The agony of having a child with a chronic and inevitably fatal illness cannot be fully appreciated by those who have never personally experienced it. Vicarious experiences are inherently limited and always incomplete. The quality and intensity of emotions are never as deep for the observer as for the participant.

Bryan Jr.'s illness and death had pushed both Anne and I toward traditional religion, I for the first time. Religion provides a happy ending, something which seems unimportant as long as the end is not imminent for oneself or for one's family and loved ones. In the case of a dying child, your own child, an idyllic hereafter not only provides a happy outcome in your own mind but, more importantly, allows you to provide, at least verbally, a happy ending for your child. At times like these, the overwhelming evidence against the existence of traditional religion becomes unfocused and unwelcome. Emotion dominates.

Tragically, the awful ordeal, for us and for Bryan Jr., could have been prevented if Anne had undergone amniocentesis in the second trimester of her pregnancy and had elected to have an abortion when the diagnosis had been made. But there was no history of cystic fibrosis in either of our families and amniocentesis does carry a small risk. Although cystic fibrosis is the most commonly recognized genetic disease in whites with one out of twenty persons carrying the gene, it still means that a carrier has only a one in twenty chance of marrying another carrier and that only one in four hundred couples will both be carriers. On the other hand, screening of the genetically engineered cells used for genetically engineered kids is rather straightforward for cystic fibrosis and is routinely employed.

We hardly ever spoke of Bryan Jr. to the other two children although Bryan III knew why he was the third and not junior. But the memory of Bryan Jr. was always with us, just below the level of consciousness. When we were alone, we would talk about him. The discussions tended to be rather clinical; it was too painful to let the conversations drift in an emotional direction. We would talk about the benefits of advances in genetic engineering and the suffering that now could be prevented.

"You didn't give your data about the reduction in genetic disease today," I commented.

"I couldn't fit it in," Anne replied.

"But it's really impressive," I continued.

"It's also a little painful to talk about," Anne added.

"I know, that's sort of my point," I went on. "Most people, particularly young housestaff don't fully understand the magnitude of how tragic it is to have a child with a chronic, fatal, disease. And now that it's preventable, it's that much more tragic."

"It would be hard to be much more tragic," Anne said seriously, and with more than a trace of sadness.

It was clear that these emotional scars would be with us for the rest of our lives. And yet you can't wish that a child of yours never happened. Once created, they're special, no matter how flawed; that's coded into our genes, too.

9

Transition Generation —
The World

The room was again packed.

"In this second seminar," Anne began, "I'm going to review the status of human genetic engineering as practiced in various countries other than the United States. Much of the data is from the Fourth World Congress on Genetic Engineering in Humans, held in Tokyo last month." Anne and I had both attended the meeting; Anne's first slide was of a classic Japanese garden.

"There are now fourteen countries with human genetic engineering programs for genetic enrichment, as opposed to genetic engineering for gene therapy," Anne continued as she showed a slide listing the fourteen countries ranked in descending order by the total number of genetically engineered infants officially reported at the time of the World Congress. The United States was first, followed by Germany, Japan, Britain, Australia, Sweden, France, Israel, Denmark, Holland, Canada, Italy, and China. Russia was listed at the bottom followed by a question mark since no official figure was available.

"What are the best estimates for Russia?" asked Dr. Oldham, department chairman. Since seminars are interruptible, there would be many questions.

"There is really very little public information," Anne replied. "Their molecular geneticists attend the various meetings, but rarely present papers and never discuss specifics. The impression, however, is that they have been active in the field for a number of years.

"Right now there are more similarities than differences among the various programs," Anne went on. "The techniques for harvesting the potential mother's ovum, for removing the native nucleus from the ovum, for inserting the donor nucleus, and for transferring the ovum, now a zygote, back to the mother's uterus are all very similar. None of the programs allow cloning and all tend to cross chromosomes from just two donors, only because crossing more than two is technically more difficult and results in a higher abortion rate."

"How do they prevent cloning?" asked one of the residents.

"It's prohibited by law in all of the countries," Anne replied. "There are a few known instances of cloning that occurred before it was illegal, but, in general, couples would prefer to have a new unique genome rather than a clone."

"What was the outcome in the clones?" the resident continued.

"The oldest one is Japanese, now eighteen," Anne answered. The donor was a famous Japanese scientist, Hideo Oihsi, who is no longer living. Although the family of the clone refuses to allow interviews or pictures, surreptitious photographs have been compared to the scientist's childhood pictures and they show a striking resemblance, like identical twins!" Anne said with a 'What would you expect?' smile. "There have also been one or two clones, there is some dispute, in Germany and Sweden," Anne went on. "Like the Japanese family, they shun publicity, but it is known that the cloned offspring closely resemble the donors."

"The programs are all sponsored by some form of a national health organization," Anne continued. The next slide was a table of the percentage of infants that were products of genetic engineering in each country. "Participation is voluntary in all of the countries. However, there are financial incentives, mainly through the tax system, in most of the countries, including the United States. Holland, Italy, and Canada currently have no financial incentives. The participation rate of couples varies among countries and does correlate to some extent with the magnitude of incentives."

"The lowest rate of participation is in Italy with six percent and the highest is in Japan with seventy seven percent," Anne said as she pointed to Japan in the table. "The United States is second at seventy three percent."

"In all fourteen countries the donors are selected by a system of regional and national committees," Anne went on. "The number of donors relative to the population of the country and the selection criteria vary somewhat from country to country. In general, the percentage of the population used for donors is a trade-off between maximizing the rate of genetic improvement and the risks of too little diversity. Those are the biological trade-offs; the exact percentage chosen is mainly a political question, which therefore requires a political answer."

"What effect do you think international economic competition will have on genetic policies?" asked Dr. Oldham.

"There was a great deal of discussion on that point at the Tokyo meeting," Anne replied. "The very high participation rate in Japan and their emphasis on business and engineering in the donors is causing great concern among American businessmen. None of the genetically engineered offspring have reached the workforce yet, but they will in a matter of a few years. Since the lag time between the time a country decides to emphasize certain traits to the time when those traits are expressed in adults is so long, it is argued that it is dangerous to wait and see what effect the policies of another country will have before instituting similar policies or counter measures."

"It seems to me," Dr. Oldham commented, "that international competition will be an ever-increasing influence in donor selection, both at home and abroad. And with no effective world government to look out for the arts and humanities, for example, some of the changes in the gene pool could be undesirable."

"I share the same concern," Anne responded. "A whole session at the World Congress was devoted to this concern. There were no easy answers." After pausing, for other comments, Anne continued in a lighter vein. "In Italy they have specific provisions for the propagation of genomes of opera stars. And there has even been discussion of propagating the genomes of cardinals and the pope. A variation on immaculate conception."

"What effect do you think the improving gene pool in the developed countries will have on the underdeveloped countries?" asked one of the medical students.

"The effects are likely to be detrimental," Anne replied. "It is too soon to see any concrete results, but presumably the gap between the developed and underdeveloped countries in technology and standard of living will widen. There is some talk of offering assistance to such countries to help them set up their own genetic improvement programs. Otherwise, they might find themselves increasingly in the position of only providing cheap labor to manufacture products that are designed and consumed in the developed countries."

"How long does it take to wash the dishes?" Anne inquired coming into the kitchen.

"Oh, yeah, the dishes," I said sheepishly. I had finished the task some time ago and had been sitting at the kitchen table lost in my own thoughts.

"It's dangerous to leave you alone," Anne chided.

"It was worth it," I answered, regaining my composure. "I've got it all figured out. How it's going to happen."

"I think I need to get back to my manuscript," Anne said with a smile.

10

Consultant to the Pentagon

I wasn't officially in the military, of course, but it felt like it, with everyone in uniforms, guards at all the gates, and all the emphasis on saluting, recognizing rank, standing erect, chest out, polished shoes, and so on.

What I hadn't counted on was spending the first two weeks doing nothing but going through security clearance, especially when I had recently undergone FBI security clearance to work at the Brookings Institution.

But this time, the CIA was running the security check. During the first couple of days in a series of interviews with various CIA agents they reviewed my entire life's history with an emphasis on obtaining the names and whereabouts of anyone with whom I had had extensive contact: teachers, childhood friends, college roommates, medical school classmates, research associates, and so on. Later, to my amazement, I found out that the CIA interviewed the majority of these individuals within a week or two.

Anne was also required to undergo interviews delving into her past. I was not allowed to attend these sessions and they won't share the results with me. I thought I might learn some details about her college beaus of whom she would occasionally remind me.

Most of the second week was kind of an indoctrination course. It included an overview of United States history and the current world political situation. Military officers gave the lectures. I must admit that this part of the security clearance was interesting and that some of the lectures were well done.

Less interesting were the personality and psychological tests given by CIA personnel. How would I react to this situation? What would I do in these circumstances? I always found myself trying to figure out what they were getting at and what answer they wanted. It was tempting to give the wrong answer just to see what would happen, but I wanted my pay check to keep coming, and I was becoming more intrigued to know what sort of assignment I had stumbled into.

When I asked why the clearance procedures were so extensive, they would only say that this was required for the position. When I asked exactly what position that was, they would only say that they couldn't tell me until I had passed the security procedures.

During the whole process the stress was on the need to maintain strict silence about my work, whatever that might turn out to be. It was of the utmost importance that I discuss it with no one, not even Anne. That was going to be hard. We really didn't keep secrets from each other. I could see it placing a strain on our marriage, at least temporarily.

My top secret clearance was finally issued. I was to join a small group at the Pentagon who were working on a project codenamed, "The Right Stuff."

The next morning I reported to a meeting room at the end of a long corridor. I showed my security card to the armed marine guard, and entered a small conference room. Inside were a one star general, a full colonel, a navy captain, and two other civilians besides myself. General Edward Abercrombie of the air force, whom I had briefly met earlier, was in charge and introduced me to the others.

"Bryan, I'd like you to meet Colonel John Gibson, Army," General Abercrombie began. "John is a biologist and in charge of research at the army's Dugway Proving Grounds in Utah. This is Captain Jack O'Reilly of the Office of Naval Research. This is Jim Randolph who's representing the National Security Council. And this is Dr. Walsh McIntyre whom you may know."

"Nice meeting you," I said as I shook the last hand. "I haven't had the opportunity to meet Dr. McIntyre before, but I certainly know him by reputation."

"Good, I hope," Dr. McIntyre said with a smug smile.

"Of course," I smiled back. Walsh McIntyre was a relatively young, say late thirties, molecular geneticist from the NIH who had the reputation of being very aggressive. What I had seen of him at national meetings left no doubt that the reputation was well deserved.

"Let me take a moment to fill Bryan in on our mission," General Abercrombie went on. "The Right Stuff is a top-secret and very sensitive project. Although we need expertise from the civilian sector, we have limited the civilian experts to two, you and Walsh, to minimize the chances of a leak. Nothing personal.

"The document you signed," he continued, "to keep everything about this project totally confidential, means exactly what it says. You will be prosecuted to the full extent of the law if there are any violations."

He stared directly at me and I nodded soberly that I understood. It was strange how the general's personality could change so quickly from genuinely human to mechanical military.

After a pause, he said quite softly, "The Central Intelligence Agency has evidence that the Russians may be using genetic engineering to build, or create, a breed of super soldiers. Our mission is to evaluate the national security risks posed by such a Russian program, assuming it exists, and to determine what steps, if any, the United States should take in response."

Even though the thought of superpower competition in genetic engineering had previously crossed my mind and I had wondered what the Pentagon had in mind for me, I was still stunned. I had expected something along the usual lines of biological warfare, that is, genetic engineering in bacteria or other microbes.

"The CIA evidence," General Abercrombie explained, "includes the fact that some of the best molecular geneticists in Russia, Drs. Igor Yevchenko and Ilya Mitrovitch, for example, have moved to the Russian Institute for Biological Warfare in Gorky."

I knew of these two. The Russian molecular geneticists were not considered the equal of those in the West, but these were certainly two of their best. They had done most of their work at the respected Institute for Biological Studies in Moscow.

"In addition," General Abercrombie continued, "the CIA has direct information from a mole inside the Institute for Biological Warfare, that the Russians are considering cloning great soldiers and officers, as well as scientists who have contributed significantly to the development of weapons systems. You can imagine the impact this could have."

"It would take years before the clones were old enough to have an impact," I observed.

"True," Walsh McIntyre interjected with an 'I've already thought of that' look. "But unless you can shorten the time needed for human maturation, once your behind, you'll stay behind."

"Our specific task," Jim Randolph said, "is to come up with a report that: one, spells out the feasibility of cloning humans; two, evaluates the possibility of using large animals, other than humans, for gestation; and three, discusses what sort of upbringing the clones should have. The report is due in six weeks, and it goes directly to the National Security Council.

For a few seconds, I just sat there staring at the rest of them, and they just stared at me. I think they were waiting for my reaction to what Jim

Randolph had just said. On the one hand I felt like saying "Thanks, but no thanks, I'm really not interested," but on the other hand, it was sort of an intellectual challenge and I really didn't believe that the United States, or Russia, would find cloning worthwhile. It was like marrying your sister, it was inherently unnatural.

"Do you really think this will happen?" I said for lack of anything better to say.

"It's basically a contingency plan," asserted Captain O'Reilly.

I'd always heard that the military had to be ready for any eventuality. In fact, I had always worried a little that their contingency plans might not be adequate and that they might not consider all the possibilities. So far I couldn't complain about this one.

"The idea," O'Reilly continued, "is to have a plan, consistent with current scientific capabilities, that can be implemented if needed. The plan will, of course, have to be periodically updated."

"Once again," General Abercrombie emphasized, "let me remind all of you that any leak of this project will result in an enormous public uproar that would probably prevent the development of the necessary contingency plans and, at the same time, result in unwarranted public anxiety regarding possible Russian activities in this area."

During the next couple of weeks we settled into a routine. Walsh, Colonel John Gibson (who turned out to be a pretty fair biologist), and I worked on various technical aspects of the report. Captain Jack O'Reilly and General Abercrombie worked on the logistics and command structure, for example, how many cloned soldiers and officers would be needed to be effective, would they be integrated into regular units or form separate elite units, would they be used in all service branches, where would their bases be located, and so on. Jim Randolph concerned himself with the number of cloned military scientists, primarily physicists, that would be needed, and our six-week deadline. Occasionally, he would prod us with some bit of evidence of Russian activities, such as a program to preserve cell lines from World War II heroes who were still living.

The answer to the basic question, could humans be cloned, was almost certainly yes; it hadn't been done yet, but animals had been cloned, and all of the medical techniques needed for cloning in man were already developed. The really difficult questions were: could you gestate human fetuses in large animals, assuming you wanted to, and how would you raise them. Periodically, I had to remind myself that this was really happening, that the military, part of our government, was really planning for the cloning of humans, even if only as a contingency.

"What about gestating the clones in women who are already in the military?" asked O'Reilly. "That might be a lot more acceptable to the public than animals."

"The public would go berserk with any of these proposals," commented McIntyre.

"Yes," Randolph said seriously, "I think you have to assume that this would have to be a classified project. That the public would not, really could not, be told about it. But if you gestated the clones in women, then you have a whole group of people who are intimately and emotionally involved. The word would definitely get out. I think it has to be gestation in animals."

"Is that technically feasible?" asked General Abercrombie. "What do our biologists say?"

"I think there is no question that it could be done," answered Walsh. "Its been done many times in animals. For reasons we don't understand, the uterus does not reject foreign proteins; otherwise reproduction would be impossible."

Walsh was referring to the fact that each human being has a different set of proteins called antigens that allow one's own immune system to recognize another individual's tissues as foreign. That is why organ transplant recipients must have their immune systems suppressed. The only exceptions to this antigenic or tissue uniqueness is identical twins who are, in fact, clones.

"Now what about raising these clones?" asked General Abercrombie.

Sometimes you got the feeling that the general didn't really take the substance of this project seriously although there was no question that he took his duties, and his position, quite seriously.

"Can you raise good soldiers outside of a family environment?" asked O'Reilly. I certainly didn't want to tackle that question.

"Clearly, only experience will answer that question definitely," said Walsh. "However, I think that a collective childhood environment, somewhat like the one posed by B. F. Skinner in *Walden Two*, might be the most practical solution. You only really need it until about age twelve, then I would think you would want them in some sort of military academy-type environment."

"We're probably talking about all males aren't we?" asked General Abercrombie.

"What happens when these clones are of legal age?" I inquired. "What about marriage, the offspring of the clones, and if the clones want to leave the service? I don't see how this whole thing will work."

"That's a legitimate conclusion for this group to reach," interjected Randolph. "However, I think you need to remember that the Russians, with their closed, authoritarian society, are not constrained the way we are. The Russians may raise their clones in a fanatical environment so that they are willing to forgo marriage, never leave the service, and take great risks with their own lives. Sort of 'biorobots.' Yet we have to compete with them."

"Another approach, maybe more realistic," Gibson said thoughtfully, "would be to clone our best physicists. A technological breakthrough like the atomic bomb, or radar, is worth a lot of divisions."

In comparison to cloning divisions of foot soldiers or scores of George Pattons, this proposal seemed utterly inoffensive. However, I could see that it had all of the same moral, ethical, legal, political, and practical problems as the broader proposal. The problems were just on a much smaller scale.

"It's much more likely that an operation on that scale could be carried out in secret," offered Gibson. "But still it probably would get out."

After several more weeks of debate and brainstorming we reached a consensus to acknowledge in the report that scientifically, at least, cloning was possible, the gestation could be carried out in large animals, and the clones could be raised in environmentally controlled groups. However, our opinion was that the operation probably could not be kept secret and that it would so enrage the public that it would be politically unacceptable.

We did provide detailed plans for implementation of full-scale cloning for military purposes as a contingency and a small program for cloning valuable scientists, again as a contingency. The report was forwarded to the National Security Council to gather dust. None of us, I think, really thought that the Russians would pursue cloning for military purposes. They would certainly risk a world opinion backlash of unprecedented proportions.

11

The Genetically
Engineered Society

When the report was finished, I was given two weeks "leave." Anne took a week off from her research job at the NIH and we drove down to the North Carolina coast. We found a cabin on the beach in an out-of-the-way place several miles from the nearest town. It was late afternoon and the weather was just right, there was a gentle breeze to temper the usual heat and humidity. As we walked along the almost deserted beach, Anne couldn't resist asking one more time.

"C'mon Bryan," Anne said with a grin. "There are no CIA agents out here. Just tell me, in general terms, what this project is all about."

"How do I know you're not working for the KGB?" I replied with feigned concern.

"You don't, that's what makes it exciting," Anne responded and then added, "Anyway, how could a pediatrician do something so evil."

"OK," I conceded. "As long as you absolutely promise not to tell anyone." Then, after a pause for effect, I continued. "We're developing this super female that the military will use to distract the enemy troops. She'll have just the right pheromones to go along with her perfect body, and …"

"Right," Anne interjected and dropped the subject.

As we continued along the beach I began to think about what the genetically engineered society of the future might be like, long after the transition phase, when having genetically engineered offspring would be second nature and culturally much more important than television, taxes, and indoor plumbing.

I imagined that Anne and I were being taken on a guided tour of this society of the future by a genetically updated Dr. Levitt. His incisive mind was unchanged, but his physical appearance was improved — he had all his hair, his nose wasn't quite so prominent, and he wasn't wearing glasses. Individually, they were all rather minor changes, but overall an impressive improvement. His personality wasn't quite as rough as I remembered it as a fellow in his lab either.

"Well what do you think?" Dr. Levitt inquired. The city was composed of nicely designed buildings, broad boulevards and walkways, and many small parks. There was no sign of the usual litter and debris. We were standing in a plaza between what looked like an office building and a broad avenue.

"You can certainly see the improvement in physical appearance," I replied struck by not only the attractiveness of the women in their prime, but also the older women as well.

"Not bad at all," added Anne. I don't think she was looking at the same specimens that I was.

The overall appearance reminded me of an exclusive athletic resort, like Vail or Aspen. The gene pool always seems better in a place like that. I was beginning to feel a bit self-conscious about my non-engineered "wild-type" appearance.

About this time I noticed that I didn't recognize the language the people were speaking. It clearly wasn't English or any of the languages I had ever come in contact with.

"What language are they speaking?" I asked Dr. Levitt.

"That's Loglan," he replied.

I recognized the name for an experimental language that had been developed to be totally logical, therefore, the name Loglan for "logical language." It had no ambiguities, one symbol for one sound, no excess verbiage, and words were spelled the way they were pronounced and vice versa. The only trouble in the past had been that no one wanted to learn a language that wasn't in use, and if no one learned it, it would never be in use.

"How did you ever get people to use it?" I asked.

"It wasn't easy," Dr. Levitt answered. "Primarily it was part of a deal to incorporate France into the United States."

"France is part of the United States?" Anne exclaimed. She had been an exchange student in France one summer during her college days and knew very well how chauvinistic the French were about their culture and particularly about their language.

"Right," Dr. Levitt went on, "it's a rather long story. There have been a lot of changes."

"Does Russia still exist?" I inquired.

"Wait a minute," Dr. Levitt interjected, raising his hand with a smile. "How about this? We'll go over to my office," he said as he motioned toward the building behind us, "and I'll fill you in on the political changes that have occurred since your time. Then this afternoon we'll visit one of the reproductive clinics. And this evening I'll take you out to dinner."

"Great," Anne commented, trying to make conversation and eye some of the genetically engineered hunks who were walking by at the same time.

On the way to Dr. Levitt's office he explained that he was the regional director for the NPGI (apparently the name hadn't changed). Upon entering his spacious modern office, I noticed that there was no secretary, or room or desk for a secretary.

"I suppose computers and electronics have replaced secretaries," I commented.

"Exactly," he replied. "More about that later."

Dr. Levitt indicated that we should sit in two chairs off to the side of the room. He sat next to us and picked up a device that reminded me of a remote control for a TV. After pushing a few buttons, a large holographic image of the earth appeared near the opposite wall. After a brief demonstration of how he could rotate the globe, enlarge any portion of it, or display the geographic distribution of population, rainfall (which they still couldn't fully control), and so on, he described the current world political situation.

"The green areas are all part of the United States," he said. "There are now eighty-seven states. Each province of Canada became a state, then the various divisions of Great Britain became states, then Germany, Denmark, Australia, and France. The motivating factors on the part of the joining countries were many, but access to genetic engineering technology was important along with other economic and security issues.

"Initially, each country that didn't already speak English had to agree to make English the primary language over a period of years," Dr. Levitt continued. "This was relatively easy, and I emphasize relatively, for Denmark and Germany since everyone in those countries was already fluent in English as their second language. Although even here there was plenty of controversy and resistance.

"The French were adamant that they would not give up their language, but they were falling behind in genetic engineering. Without state-of-the-art genetic engineering, they couldn't hope to compete technologically and economically in international trade, and their standard of living was suffering accordingly. After years and years of negotiating, it was finally agreed that France would join the enlarged United States and that over a fifty-year period Loglan would become the primary language for everyone."

"Actually, I'm amazed that all the English speakers agreed to give up English just so they could strike a deal with the French," Anne said.

"Well, in fact, adopting Loglan had been talked about for a long time," Dr. Levitt replied. "The United States had already annexed most of the English speaking countries. It was felt that the switch would allow possible future incorporation of countries like Japan.

"In addition, Loglan is so much easier to learn that our children spend, or waste, much less time learning it than they used to spend learning English, which, of course, is a relatively illogical language and breaks the rules as often as it follows them. By sixth grade they have mastered all of the grammar and rhetoric of Logan and no more language classes are required. Of course, genetic engineering has significantly improved the language centers of the brain and is responsible for part of the more rapid mastery of language.

"But I'm digressing," he interrupted himself. "The United States has annexed all of the countries now shown in green." With a push of a button all of the other current United States was displayed in green. It included Ireland, New Zealand, Austria, Italy, Spain, Holland, Belgium, Austria, and Israel.

"Negotiations with Japan, India, Norway, Sweden, Portugal, Mexico, and the Philippines are ongoing," he added.

"And what about Russia?" I asked.

"The Russians have moved in the same direction," Dr. Levitt replied. "They have officially annexed many of the Eastern European countries. They are negotiating with Cuba, much to the United States' dismay, and Vietnam. Overall you can see that the United States has grown more than Russia."

"What has happened to the underdeveloped countries?" Anne inquired.

"Unfortunately, the economic gap between them and the developed countries has increased significantly," Dr. Levitt responded. "Their gene pool has benefited very little from genetic engineering. The United States has a small assistance program for underdeveloped countries, but most of their governments have shown no sustained interest. Increasingly, the underdeveloped countries act as sweat shops that manufacture goods for the developed countries.

"Let's go over to the Reproductive Clinic," Dr. Levitt said looking at the time. "And I'll show you the progress we've made."

As we walked to the clinic Dr. Levitt explained that for some time they had had the technology to quickly sequence an entire genome and to insert or delete genes at specific sites. In addition, by studying the physical, intellectual, and behavioral characteristics of literally millions of individuals, they now had extensive knowledge of the results that could be expected from the presence of single genes or combinations of genes. In theory, and to a large extent in practice, they could design humans to specification.

When we arrived at the Reproductive Clinic, I was amazed to see that it wasn't just a few rooms, but a whole building, a rather large building.

"This clinic serves a population of approximately half a million people," Dr. Levitt explained. "In addition to the reproductive medicine specialists and molecular geneticists, it houses the anthropologists and psychologists who do the follow-up evaluations on everyone living in this region."

We took the elevator to the top floor and entered the office of the clinic director, none other than Dr. Walsh McIntyre. Like Dr. Levitt there had been obvious improvements in his physical appearance, he didn't look as unathletic as before and his skin color was more robust.

And like everyone else in this genetically engineered society, he seemed to have no need for glasses.

"I've asked Dr. McIntyre to give you a summary of how our genetics and reproductive program works," Dr. Levitt said. "I'll come back and pick you up at about five and we'll go out to dinner."

We thanked Dr. Levitt and sat down around a small conference table.

"I understand that Dr. Levitt has explained that we have the ability to alter or synthesize the genes within a genome to any specifications," Walsh began. "This has allowed us to develop a program in which new individuals are truly engineered, not just uncontrolled crosses between selected genomes as in the past. The key points in our program can be summarized as follows: one, all females are engineered to be sterile; two, all offspring are designed at clinics like this one; and three, follow-up studies are done on all individuals at periodic intervals throughout their lifetime."

Walsh certainly hadn't lost his talent for coming quickly to the point.

"Certainly sounds very scientific," Anne commented. "How do you make all females sterile?"

"All of our females are born, engineered that is, without fallopian tubes," Walsh replied with a smile of satisfaction.

"I'm not sure I would want my daughter engineered that way," Anne responded.

"That is the way everyone felt initially," Walsh continued. "Although everyone agreed that there would be significant advantages if unwanted pregnancies could be prevented in the first place, and if genetic counseling and genetic enhancement could be provided for each wanted pregnancy, there was a reluctance to engineer sterility into females or males. So initially an antibody technique was used. At age four, just prior to school, when the children were given their vaccines for various infectious diseases, the females were injected with an antigen found on all sperm that induced their immune systems to produces antibodies. The presence of circulating antibodies to all sperm then rendered them sterile."

"Sounds similar to infertility in prostitutes," I commented. It had been known for some time that prostitutes, exposed to numerous different sperm antigens, developed antibodies that resulted in an increased frequency of infertility.

"Right, but we don't emphasize the similarity," said Walsh. "Anyway, this technique was publicly acceptable and allowed the institution of a controlled genetic enhancement program. With time people became used to the lack of need for birth control and to the idea of having their offspring engineered. Eventually it was found simpler to just delete the genes that code for fallopian tube development. Now we only use the antigen approach on immigrants."

"I hope women still gestate their offspring," Anne said.

"Yes, that hasn't changed," Walsh replied. "Serious consideration was given, at various times, to using large animals instead of humans, but there was strong opposition from men and women alike. It would have eliminated the small but definite health risk to women, and it would have eliminated the adverse effects that pregnancy can have on a woman's appearance. However, the bonding aspects of gestating were felt to be too important, both for the prospective mother and for the prospective father, to tamper with."

"Do mothers still nurse their infants?" Anne asked.

"That hasn't changed either," Walsh answered. "It's one of the basic instincts that we felt it would be unwise to change. Sort of like the urge to breath, we try very hard to avoid changing those genes."

"Do you know which genes control those instincts?" I asked.

"To some extent," Walsh replied. "Overtime we have noted that there are a group of genes that are different in those few women who have little urge to nurse."

"Now that you have total control over reproduction, I suppose there are criteria that have to be met before a woman can be impregnated." Anne inquired.

"Well, we still have a democracy," Walsh answered with a smile. "So all the rules have majority approval. Congress has set three criteria for procreation. First, a woman or man must be married. There is ongoing controversy on this point, but the vast majority of citizens have always supported this rule. Second, the couple must meet minimum financial criteria. Income from almost any single full-time job is sufficient, approximately ninety-five percent of adults would fall into this category."

"What about people like artists?" Anne asked. "Do they have difficulty qualifying?"

"Probably a little more so than others," Walsh replied. "But it's easier than in the past. If they can demonstrate skill, they usually can get a government stipend. It's a bit like getting a research grant. You submit a proposal and your CV, and the application is reviewed and acted on by the National Arts Council. Each year Congress decides on the total amount of money that will be spent on stipends for the arts and how the money will be distributed among broad categories: music, dance, painting, sculpture, et cetera.

"There is a third criterion," Walsh went on. "There must be no evidence of significant mental instability in either prospective parent. The couples follow-up records are reviewed, primarily the social and psychological data."

"That sounds like a great area for controversy," Bryan commented.

"Your right," Walsh continued. "By law no more than two percent of couples can be rejected for parenthood on this ground. This prevents the reviewers from being too finicky. And those rejected can appeal the decision to the NPGI Review Board and in the courts. Since most of the genes that predispose for aberrant behavior, such as criminality or alcoholism, have already been eliminated, the undesirable behavior that we encounter is more environmentally based."

"It sounds like it's probably a stigma not to have children," I said. "People assume you're mentally unstable."

"That is an unintended consequence of this criterion," Walsh agreed. "But it's always been a stigma to varying degrees not to have children."

"How many children do each couple get, two?" asked Anne.

"In general, yes," Walsh answered. "One boy and one girl, in the order of their choosing. Since a few couples chose not to have children and a few more do not meet the minimum criteria and are not allowed to have children, the population would gradually decline if there were not some compensating mechanism. There are two mechanisms that allow for adjustments in the population size. One is immigration, and the other is raising a child with a genome selected by the NPGI."

"You mean all genomes are not selected by the NPGI?" Anne inquired.

"Right, I'll come back to that in a minute," Walsh replied. "The NPGI genomes represent combinations of genes that the NPGI has reason to believe will result in superior individuals although they are combinations that are significantly different from previously studied genomes. There has always been a waiting list for these genomes because they allow couples to have more than two children and because these genomes usually turn out to be exceptional children."

"So where do the genomes come from for the 'usual and customary' two children?" Anne persisted.

"Couples are allowed to use their own genes," Walsh answered, "assuming they don't include any genes on the prohibited list. That's a list of genes that have been determined to be undesirable. Included are all known genes that code for genetic disease, behavioral abnormalities, low intelligence, and physical inconveniences such as near-sightedness. If the couple's genomes contain none of these, they may even have their genomes randomly crossed the old-fashioned way!" Walsh smiled at the thought that any sane person would want to create their progeny and heirs that way.

"Usually, couples start with their own genomes," Walsh went on, "delete any genes that have been placed on the prohibited list since they themselves were born, and create a new genome by choosing the best genes from both of their own genomes. In addition, there is a large array of genes, sort of standard parts, which are available through the NPGI that can be incorporated into your offspring's genome."

"Amazing," I exclaimed. "How long does it take you to sequence a genome with its twenty thousand plus genes?"

"Twenty thousand, eight hundred and fifty-three genes, to be exact," said Walsh basking in the accumulated knowledge of the decades. "Currently, we have it automated to the point that it only takes about ten minutes to get a complete printout with all prohibited genes flagged, of course."

"And you can synthesize any combination you want?" I asked.

"Right," Walsh replied, "almost as fast as a genome can be sequenced. Well, not quite that fast, but fast enough. There's no longer any need to save cell lines." Walsh was obviously enjoying the chance to show off the state of their technology. "The really hard part was not the sequencing and synthesizing of the genes, but figuring out what they coded for, individually and in the essentially unlimited possible combinations. That was, and is, the tedious, messy part that keeps a lot of medical people, particularly psychologists, busy. Everyone gets an in-depth interview every five years."

"Do you have pictures of the various physical features that couples can choose from?" Anne asked.

"It's all on computers," Walsh answered. "You can mix and match, sort of like that old children's game Mr. Potato Head."

"How do you control height?" I wondered out loud thinking of the fact that while I certainly hadn't noticed any short people, there weren't any giants either. "I can see that it wouldn't be a problem if everyone wanted to maximize intelligence, or say good looks, but how do you keep everyone from wanting their children to be just a little taller than everyone else's?"

"Fairly simple," Walsh said. "NPGI recommended an average height of one hundred eighty-five centimeters, approximately six foot one, for men and one hundred seventy-three centimeters, approximately five eight, for women. After some debate, Congress adopted the recommendations with the condition that the changes be gradually instituted over one generation, twenty-five years. Of course we don't hit those targets exactly all the time, but currently ninety-five percent of individuals are within plus or minus two centimeters of the mark."

"So couples don't get any choice in height," Anne commented.

"Right," Walsh said.

"How do you handle breast size?" I asked, smiling at my play on words. Anne looked mildly annoyed.

"We just eliminated A and D cups," Walsh responded returning my smile.

"Everyone's in the B to C range. Parents have a choice here, and the preference is about fifty-fifty."

"What has happened to IQ?" Anne asked. "Is everyone a genius?" I think she was trying to redirect the line of questioning.

"Well, of course, the IQ is much higher now than it used to be," Walsh answered. "On the old scale our current average would be about 160 and the range is approximately 140 to 180, a significantly narrower range than before. So almost everyone is a genius by the old standards. But, since these things are very relative, no greater percentage of individuals feels superior now than before although, perhaps, fewer feel disadvantaged."

"Have you ever tried to reproduce any of the historical greats like Bach, or Einstein, or Gauss?" Anne inquired.

"That information appears to be lost forever, Walsh said thoughtfully. "We were able to sequence the genomes of some exceptional individuals whose cell lines were preserved during the late twentieth century before routine sequencing was practiced."

Just then Dr. Levitt returned to take Anne and me to dinner. Walsh declined Dr. Levitt's invitation to join us. After Anne and I thanked Walsh for his overview of the NPGI, the three of us headed down the street to one of Dr. Levitt's favorite restaurants.

The restaurant had an old English look. Underneath the name, Yorkshire Inn, in small letters was the phrase "Perfect Food for the Perfect Genome." A rather odd mixture of the old and new I thought.

"Well, what do you think of our genetics and reproduction programs?" Dr. Levitt asked as a waiter guided us to an out-of-the-way table.

"Technologically very impressive," I replied.

"It seems to be a fairly reasonable combination of individual freedoms and societal needs," Anne added.

"We've tried to maximize individual choice with respect to offspring at the same time we've tried to incorporate all of the benefits of genetic engineering," Dr. Levitt commented.

"In many ways couples have a lot more choice about their offspring than they used to," I asserted.

"Very true," Dr. Levitt agreed. "Couples spend enormous amounts of time pondering their own sequences and the NPGI catalogues of available genes before finally deciding on the genomes for their progeny. The stands at the supermarket checkout counters are full of magazines on the subject."

"I can imagine," I replied. "Now that you've increased the prevalence of the advantageous genes and eliminated the harmful genes, where do you go from here?"

"That's a difficult problem," Dr. Levitt answered. "Initially, it was easy to make progress. Many deleterious genes had been identified before we could engineer them out of a genome. Once we had the engineering capability, we pretty much eliminated them in one generation. Then we focused on determining more subtle genetic effects, like the influence of various genes on intelligence, artistic talents, behavior, and so forth. That task is still unfinished, and considering the number of possible combinations within a total genome, may never be completely finished. But we certainly understand the broad outlines.

"Now we're faced with either a relatively stable gene pool or testing experimental genes." Dr. Levitt paused and looked at Bryan and Anne to ascertain that they understood what he was saying.

"You mean synthesizing genes not currently found in the gene pool that have not been known to exist before and incorporating them into a genome?" Anne asked.

"Right," Dr. Levitt replied. "The only other alternative for further improvement in the gene pool is to wait for random mutations in zygotes from cosmic radiation. And, of course, the vast majority of those mutations will be deleterious."

"Who makes decisions like that?" I asked.

"Congress makes them," Dr. Levitt answered. "But the debate can go on forever. It's obviously the ultimate step in genetic engineering. To this point we've really just been selecting from among available genes, favoring the propagation of some genes and preventing the propagation of others. We've substituted selection by man for natural selection and, in the process, enormously increased the rate of change in the gene pool. So far, the benefits have clearly outweighed the risks."

"I would think the chances of making a random change that resulted in improvement would be one in a million or less," I commented.

"That's probably right," Dr. Levitt agreed.

"It seems unlikely Congress would want to pursue such a program with odds like that, moral questions aside," I said.

"I think the only thing that would make the public feel that it was worthwhile is some sort of threat or competitive pressure from outside the United States," Dr. Levitt added.

"To change the subject a bit," Anne interjected, "is everyone's genome public information, or are they kept confidential?"

"They're like tax returns," Dr. Levitt responded. "The government has all the information, the information is analyzed, and general conclusions are released to the public, but individual genomes are confidential. However, individuals know their own genomes just like they know their own tax returns, and they may give that information to their physicians just like they give financial data to their accountant."

"And you could compare genomes with a close friend?" Anne inquired with a smile.

"Right," Dr. Levitt replied. "Just like a tax return."

"Is anyone's genome classified?" I asked, probably as a reflex from my exposure to top-secret projects at the Pentagon.

"Yes, the government has the right to classify a person's genome for security reasons," Dr. Levitt replied, more seriously. "This happens occasionally in cases of great physicists, mathematicians, molecular biologists, or generals. It then becomes illegal for that individual to disclose his genome although he may already have done so in the past. We've had a few cases of persons with classified genomes who have been kidnapped, temporarily, by foreign agents for the purpose of obtaining blood samples for sequencing."

"Are you classified?" I asked Dr. Levitt.

"The answer to that is classified," Dr. Levitt smiled.

"It sounds like being classified is equivalent to winning the Nobel Prize," Anne joked.

"Not exactly," Dr. Levitt responded. "The president's genome is classified, not so much to guard his strengths, but to prevent hostile parties from exploiting his genetic weaknesses."

"An enormous number of people must be employed by the NPGI," I commented.

"The Department of Genetics has the second largest number of government employees after the Department of Defense," Dr. Levitt responded. "Most are involved in collecting and analyzing data in the ongoing effort to relate the chemical structure of genes to their expression in the whole individual." Just then our waiter, young and obviously genetically well endowed, brought us our meals.

"I assume he has a genius IQ," I said. "Why does he wait on tables?"

"Remember, it's all relative," Dr. Levitt replied. "In this society he doesn't feel like a genius. And he will probably wait on tables for only a few years while he's young, maybe to put himself through college. And, of course, none of our jobs are as tedious as in the past because of continued progress in automation. Our robots are quite sophisticated. They can perform defined tasks, such as preparing most foods, without difficulty."

"I also felt like he was staring at me," I added.

"I was hoping you wouldn't notice," Dr. Levitt answered smiling. "I think it was your ears, the left one sticks out more than the right one - we're not used to that sort of minor defect any more."

"I see," I said as I self-consciously touched my left ear. And then to change the subject asked. "What has happened to religious beliefs?"

"There has been a clear trend toward humanism and a focus on ethical behavior, along the lines of what Einstein called the third level of religion," Dr. Levitt replied. He was referring to Einstein's classification of religions into three levels. The first and most primitive was characterized by worship of animate or physical gods, usually more than one. The second, and higher level, was characterized by worship of a single, non-physical spiritual god and teachings with a moral basis. The third, and most advanced level, did not involve the worship of any physical or spiritual being, but was focused on understanding the physical laws of the universe and determining the optimal ethical and moral relationships among humans. The latter are acknowledged to be relationships that must be decided by man himself, and that may vary from generation to generation depending on circumstances."

"Basically a continuation of the process already underway before," I said.

"Right," Dr. Levitt agreed. "In general, man has continued to accumulate knowledge and to use that knowledge to increase his control over his environment and, now, over the makeup of his progeny, if not himself."

"I think we better head back to the cabin," Anne said. The sun was setting and a breeze had come up.

"The sunset's great," I offered.

"As if you've noticed," Anne replied with a smile.

All too soon the peaceful, pleasant week on the North Carolina coast ended and we were back in Washington, DC, back to the world of genomes created by chance, genomes that carried mostly mediocre genes along with a few of the best genes, and almost always, a few defective genes. To a world full of physical and mental dysfunction, let alone imperfections. To disease, crime, child abuse, and personal misery. To a world of individuals condemned to spend their one and only life drawing instructions from flawed blueprints.

12

Decision to Go Ahead

As we walked up to the door of our townhouse, after the long drive back from the coast, a man got out of a nearby parked car and hurried up to me.

"Are you Dr. Bryan Kenton?" he inquired in a serious, businesslike fashion.

"Yes," I replied wondering how I was going to dispense with this salesman.

"I'm Agent Hendricks of the FBI," he said as he showed me his identification. "I have a top-secret letter for you." He handed me the letter and left. Evidently he had been staked out in front of our house for some time.

After going inside I opened the letter. It simply said:

Dear Dr. Kenton:
There is an urgent meeting of The Right Stuff project tomorrow morning at 0800 hours in Conference Room 108A.
General Abercrombie

I had told several members of the committee that we would be at the coast for only one of the two weeks I had off because that was all the time Anne could take.

"What's that all about?" Anne asked.

"Got me," I replied. "I have to be back to work tomorrow morning."

"Must be pretty important if they have an FBI agent wait outside the house ready to hand it to you the minute you get home," Anne said.

"Better be, for interrupting my vacation," I added.

Shortly after 0800 hours, when everyone had arrived, General Abercrombie proceeded to explain the reason for the urgent meeting.

"We have new intelligence reports that bear on The Right Stuff project," the general began in a serious tone of voice. "The CIA has reliable information that the Russians are going ahead with genetic engineering in humans. They're planning to develop superior genomes for physicists, military officers, and large numbers of soldiers. The genomes will be gestated in human females and raised in communal military communities."

At this point Abercrombie paused and looked around the table to be sure that we all understood the implications of what he was saying.

"How certain is the CIA?" asked Captain O'Reilly.

"Quite certain, ninety percent certain," General Abercrombie replied.

"Do you think they have the technical capability?" Colonel Gibson asked of no one in particular.

"It's not that difficult," Walsh McIntyre responded somewhat condescendingly.

"So what do we do now?" I asked.

"There are basically three options," General Abercrombie replied. "We could do nothing. We could have a national debate on how to respond. Or we could proceed with implementing our own program without a public debate."

"Are we to decide that?" I asked incredulously.

"No, its been decided," General Abercrombie continued. "The president, the secretary of defense, the chairman of the Joint Chiefs of Staff, and the National Security Council all feel that we can't afford to get behind in this area. They have decided that to do nothing could be disastrous. They also feel that a public debate would be very lengthy and that a positive decision would only come after it was clear that this technology worked and that it was a real threat, and by then we would be many years behind. Consequently, they have decided to proceed at once."

"What happens when the public finds out?" I asked. "There will be an enormous outcry."

"The president is willing to take that chance," General Abercrombie replied. "As the Russian program progresses, he feels that the wisdom of a US program will become more and more obvious."

"What are the guidelines?" Captain O'Reilly inquired.

"Jim, could you give the group an overview of our guidelines?"

Jim Randolph, of the National Security Council, opened a folder lying in front of him. "The guidelines are as follows: One, this committee, at least initially, will oversee the project under the same code name, The Right Stuff. Two, the project will have the highest possible secrecy classification. Three, the project will be based at the army's Dugway Biological Research Center in Utah. Four, the project will initially focus on producing a limited number of genomes likely to result in superior military officers and scientists essential to the national defense. Five, the genomes will be gestated in female military volunteers. And six, the progeny will be raised initially by the gestating volunteer and later in special schools that will provide the appropriate military or scientific training."

"Will the genomes be clones?" Walsh McIntyre asked pointedly.

"That has yet to be decided," General Abercrombie replied.

"I certainly agree with the decision to base the project at Dugway," Colonel Gibson commented. "I assume there will be adequate funding."

"You can assume that, Colonel," General Abercrombie responded with a trace of irritation. Then after a pause, he continued, "I know that this is a significant change in mission and that some of you may not feel comfortable in continuing with the project. Between now and tomorrow morning I want each of you to decide whether you want to continue. Starting tomorrow we will begin working on the details of implementing the president's decision. So that's all for today; we'll meet again in this room at 0800 hours tomorrow morning. And remember, nothing gets said of this project outside of this room."

On the way home my mind was busy thinking of many things.

I thought of how all branches of science had spawned technologies that could be used for both good and evil. Mathematics is the soul of computers, and computers have certainly improved man's lot. The CT scanner in medicine, which could not exist without computers, allows painless and quick evaluation of internal organs, a process that previously required surgery. But at the same time, computers are used to gather, store, and retrieve ever-increasing amounts of personal data on every individual. While abuses of the data in the United States have been limited to endless mail, phone, and email solicitations, in other countries the computer is used as an electronic leash between an oppressive government and its citizens. And there are, of course, military uses of computers and more recently attempts by Russia to interfere with our presidential election.

Advances in physics have resulted in the discovery of nuclear energy, which in turn, gives rise to potentially clean, inexpensive, and inexhaustible power supplies on the one hand and atomic weapons on the other. Chemistry is no different. The same techniques that allow us to synthesize wonder drugs can also be used to design toxic compounds for chemical warfare.

Somehow, naively, I had thought of biology as different, even though the biological world is full of predators and prey. Man's exploitation of biology and biotechnology have come relatively late. On the negative side there have been the mostly unused bacterial toxins stockpiled by the military. Now, the age of innocence for biotechnology would end.

I thought of what H. G. Wells said: "Civilization is a race between education and catastrophe." Somehow "education" no longer seemed like quite the right word. It ignores the pervasive constraints that our genetic makeup places on ever achieving optimal behavior – constraints that, for some reason, are very hard to see although the evidence is visible all around us. The problem most likely stems from each individual's misguided feeling of self-control. Perhaps "genetic enhancement" should be substituted for, or at least added to "education" in H. G. Wells' aphorism.

For my part, I would call Dr. Levitt in the morning and see if his offer to have me back in the lab any time still stood. It was an easy decision, even though I had twinges of unpatriotic feelings. But there would be plenty of willing talent to uphold the United States' end in this new sphere of superpower competition. I was sure of that.

Then I saw a guy on the street corner selling flowers. I almost never gave Anne flowers. Suddenly, I felt a need to be close to Anne. The morning's events had somehow released an intense emotional feeling. I felt cutoff from the rest of the world more than usual.

A singular and historic step was about to be taken. For most of recorded history and before, it has been dogma that the gods created man; but during the last few thousand years, with the rise of science and the expansion of man's knowledge, many began to suspect that, in fact, it was man who had created the gods. Now with the relatively recent, but enormous advances in molecular biology, it seemed inevitable that man will create man.

Milestones in the Genetic Engineering of Man

Date	Event
~4.4 billion years BC	Life originates on earth.
~200,000 years BC	Homo sapiens evolve.
~70,000 years BC	Homo sapiens sapiens develop culture, that allows for the accumulation of knowledge.
Early 1600s	Regnier de Graaf, a Dutch scientist, recognized that the essential element of conception is the union of the sperm with the egg.
Late 1800s	Gregor Mendel, a Moravian monk, using the garden pea demonstrated the statistical nature of inheritance and described dominant and recessive traits.

| 1903 | Walter S. Sutton and Theodor Boveri independently proposed the chromosome theory of heredity, that is that the factors or genes responsible for heredity resides in the tiny strands called chromosomes that are found in the nuclei of cells. |

| 1933 | Thomas H. Morgan received the Nobel Prize for work in the fruit fly that established that genes are arranged linearly along chromosomal strands. |

| 1953 | M. H. F. Wilkins, F. H. C. Crick, and J. D. Watson proposed the double-helix model of DNA which explains DNA replication. This work led to a Nobel Prize in 1962. |

| 1966 | H. Gorbind Khorana established the complete genetic code, the correlation of base sequences in DNA to amino acids, the building blocks of proteins. He received the Nobel Prize in 1968. |

| 1970 | Hamilton Smith and Daniel Nathans discovered and applied the first restriction enzymes, enzymes that cut DNA at specific sites. The work was awarded a Nobel Prize in 1978. |

1972	Janet Mertz and Ron Davis used a joining enzyme to combine DNA fragments.
1977	Walter Gilbert and Fred Sanger independently developed powerful methods of sequencing or mapping DNA. They shared the 1980 Nobel Prize.
1982	R. D. Palmiter and colleagues created supermice by injecting the growth hormone gene of a rat into fertilized mouse eggs. The mice grew to be twice as large as normal mice.
2015	Chinese scientists successfully used genetic engineering in a human zygote.
?	A national program of genetic enhancement in man is begun.

Glossary and Definitions

Abortion Giving birth to a fetus before the time of viability, e.g. before twenty weeks of gestation. A spontaneous abortion is a natural abortion that is not induced and is referred to as a miscarriage in lay terms. A therapeutic abortion is one that is induced because the pregnancy is a threat to the mother's health. An elective abortion is an induced abortion that is performed for reasons other than the mother's health, usually for social or economic reasons.

Allele Alternative forms of a gene found at the same site on homologous chromosomes. For example, the gene for eye color has two alleles: brown and blue.

Amino acid Small organic molecules that are the building blocks for proteins. Human proteins are composed of sequences of twenty different amino acids. Each amino acid has a carboxyl (-COOH) end and an amino end ($-NH_2$). Proteins are constructed by chemically combining the carboxyl end of one amino acid to the amino end of another amino acid.

Amniocentesis A procedure in which a needle is introduced into the gestational sac through the mother's abdomen in order to obtain a sample of amniotic fluid. The fluid is usually analyzed for diagnostic purposes.

Antigen Molecule or a portion of a molecule that is capable of stimulating the body's immune system to produce antibodies against it. The antibodies then bind to the antigen.

Antibody Proteins made by cells of the body's immune system which bind to and inactivate other substances (antigens), generally introduced from outside the body.

Autosome Any chromosome other than the sex chromosomes. Man has forty-four autosomal chromosomes (twenty-two pairs) and two sex chromosomes (one pair).

Chromosomes Large, thread-like, molecules that are found in the nucleus. Each chromosome consists of DNA, which contains the genetic code or information, and protein which gives structure to the molecule and helps regulate activity.

Clone Cells or organisms that have the same genetic material. An example is identical twins.

Conception Becoming pregnant. Fertilization of the ovum by the sperm followed by implantation of the fertilized ovum (now a zygote) in the uterus.

Co-dominance When both of two different alleles are expressed. An example is the AB blood type. If an individual possesses type A on one chromosome and type B on the homologous chromosome, his red blood cells will express both A and B proteins and he will be type AB.

Congenital Traits, conditions, or diseases that are present at birth. The cause may be genetic as in the case of hemophilia and Down syndrome or it may be environmental as in phocomelia, short extremities, which is secondary to maternal ingestion of thalidomide during pregnancy.

CRISPR/Cas9 CRISPR is an acronym for Clustered Regularly Interspaced Short Palindromic Repeats and Cas9 is a nuclease enzyme. The name refers to a molecular complex discovered in the immune system of bacteria that can be used in cells, including human cells, to relatively easily change DNA at specific sites in genes. This molecular system, and others like it, has the potential to revolutionize genetic engineering.

Cytoplasm The material within cells in which the nucleus and organelles such as mitochondria and ribosomes are imbedded. It has no discernible structure microscopically, but may be organized at the molecular level.

Dizygotic fraternal twins Twins formed from genetically different zygotes, i.e. fertilized eggs. Fraternal twins are no more alike than other brothers and sisters.

DNA Abbreviation for deoxyribonucleic acid. Composed of sequences of nucleotides that code the genetic information.

Dominant A trait that is expressed whether the individual has only one or two copies of the allele. An example is the allele for brown eye color.

Enzyme A protein that acts as catalyst in biological reactions. Like all catalysts, enzymes speed up reactions without being consumed by the reaction.

Eugenics Refers to improvement of the gene pool of man, animals, or plants by selective breeding. The word was coined by Sir Francis Galton, cousin of Charles Darwin.

FDA The Food and Drug Administration, usually referred to as the FDA, is a federal agency in the Department of Health and Human Services. It is responsible for regulating pharmaceuticals, cosmetics, and medical equipment.

Gamete The germ cells of an individual, sperm in males and ova in females. A sperm and an ovum combine to form a zygote, which develops into a new individual.

Gene A section of a DNA molecule that codes for the synthesis of a specific protein. It is typically hundreds or thousands of nucleotides long.

Gene pool The sum of all genes contained by members of a given population. The population may be of a geographical, national, racial, or ethnic nature.

Genome The total genetic makeup of an individual. Often referred to as genotype.

Genotype The exact genetic composition of an individual. The expression of the genotype in the individual, i.e. phenotype, will vary with environmental factors.

Gestation Development of the fetus within the mother's uterus. Requires an average of nine months or forty weeks in humans.

Heterozygote An individual who possesses two different alleles of one gene. An example would be an individual with type AB blood.

Homologous chromosomes Chromosomes that pair during cell division and contain identical loci for genes.

Homozygote An individual who possesses identical alleles at a particular loci on homologous chromosomes.

Karyotype The number, size, and shape of an individual's chromosomes. Generally refers to their appearance in a photomicrograph after they have been stained in a standard fashion.

Locus The location of a gene on a chromosome. A gene will have identical positions on homologous chromosomes.

Miscarriage The lay term for abortion, specifically a spontaneous expulsion of a fetus before it is viable.

Monozygotic Individuals derived from the same original cell such as identical twins. These individuals will have identical genomes.

Multifactorial Traits that are controlled by multiple genes such as height and intelligence.

Mutation A change in genetic material. It may consist of a single chemical change in one gene or a change in the number or structure of chromosomes. A mutation that occurs in a gamete will be inherited by any individual who develops from that gamete whereas a mutation that occurs in a somatic cell cannot be passed to another individual.

NIH The National Institutes of Health, usually referred to as the NIH, is a federal agency within the Department of Health and Human Services. It is responsible for the federal research effort in the biomedical sciences. It conducts a large research program of its own on its campus in Bethesda, Maryland and supports a much larger amount of medical research at medical schools across the country through the grant mechanism.

NPGI National Program for Genetic Improvement, a possible future governmental agency that would administer and coordinate the federal programs for genetic engineering in man.

Nucleotide The building block of DNA and the smallest unit of genetic code. Human DNA is made up of sequences of four different nucleotides: thymidine, cytosine, adenosine, and guanine. Each nucleotide is made up of a purine or pyrimidine base, a pentose sugar moiety, and a phosphate group.

Nucleus A membrane enclosed structure within the cell that contains the chromosomes and, thus, the genetic information.

Organism Any complete biological entity.

Ovum The female gamete, or egg. Single cell structures that are released from the ovaries on a monthly basis. When fertilized by a sperm, a new individual is formed.

Phenotype The appearance of an individual, the sum result of the interaction of the individual's genome and his environment.

Protein Large complex organic molecules composed of hundreds or thousands of amino acids. In general, each gene codes for one protein.

Recessive A trait that is expressed only when two of its alleles are present, that is when the individual is homozygous for the trait. An example is the eye color blue.

Regression to the mean The tendency for exceptional characteristics that are genetically determined in a multifactorial manner, i.e. high or low intelligence, not to breed true. That is, the offspring tend to be more average than parents with respect to exceptional traits.

RNA Abbreviation for ribonucleic acid. Similar in chemical structure to DNA, but with different functions. One type, messenger-RNA, transcribes genetic information from DNA in the nucleus and transfers the information to the cytoplasm where it serves as the template for protein synthesis. Another type, transfer RNA, transfers specific amino acids to the messenger RNA for incorporation into protein.

Sequence The process of determining the nucleotide sequence and thus the genetic constitution of an individual's genome.

Sex chromosomes The chromosomes that determine whether an individual is a male (XY) or a female (XX).

Sex-linked Genes carried on the sex chromosomes. Since the Y chromosome carries few genes, the term is often used synonymously with the term X-linked. Hemophilia and color blindness are examples.

Somatic Refers to all cells in the body other than the reproductive cells or gametes.

Sperm Male gametes that are produced in the testes and carried in the semen into the female genital tract at the time of sexual intercourse. When a sperm fertilizes an ovum, a new individual is formed.

Transcription The process of transferring genetic information from DNA to messenger-RNA.

Translation The process of producing proteins from the genetic information contained in messenger RNA.

Vestigial Said of an organ or structure that is fully developed and functional in lower life forms but, through evolution, is either not fully developed or functional in higher life forms. Examples of vestigial organs in man include the appendix of the large intestine and the gallbladder of the biliary tract.

X-linked Genes carried on the X chromosomes. An abnormal gene on the X chromosome in the male will always be expressed. In the female, because cells randomly express genetic information from one or the other of the two X chromosomes present, an abnormal gene must be present on both X chromosomes before the condition is expressed. This phenomenon explains why some diseases, such as hemophilia, are rare in females.

Zygote The fertilized ovum. The result after the sperm penetrates the ovum. The first cell of the new individual.

Related Readings

<u>Novels Dealing with the Use of Science and Technology to Alter Society</u>

1. Huxley, Aldous: *Brave New World*. New York: Harper & Row, 1932.
2. Skinner BF: *Walden Two*. New York: MacMillan Company, 1948.
3. Orwell G: *1984*. New York: Harcourt Brace Jovanovich, 1949.

<u>Essays on Human Nature and the Human Condition</u>

1. Einstein Albert: *The World As I See It*. New York: Philosophical Library, 1949.
2. Thomas Lewis: *Lives of a Cell: Notes of a Biology Watcher*. New York: Bantam Books, 1975.

<u>The Physical and Emotional Burden of Genetic Abnormalities</u>

1. Deford F: *Alex: The Life of a Child*. New York: New American Library, 1984.

The Science of Genetics

1. Watson JD, Tooze J, and Kurtz DT: *Recombinant DNA: A Short Course.* New York: Scientific American Books, 1983.
2. Emery AEH: *Elements of Human Genetics.* Edinburgh: Churchill Livingstone, 1983.
3. "Identical Twins Reared Apart - News and Comment." *Science* 207: 1323-1328, 1980.
4. Cyranoski D, Reardon S: News. *Nature,* 22 April, 2015.
5. Nussbaum RL, McInnes RR, and Huntington FW: *Thompson & Thompson Genetics in Medicine.* 8th ed, Philadelphia: Elsevier, 2016.

Copyright Page

" Last Slide" (page 12): From *Recombinant DNA: Genes and Genomes 3e* by James D. Watson, et al. Copyright 2007 by W.H. Freeman. All rights reserved. Used by permission of the publishers.

About the Author

William C. Klingensmith III grew up near Pittsburgh, Pennsylvania, attended Cornell University in Ithaca, New York and then Cornell's College of Medicine in New York City. He completed an internship in medicine at University of Oregon School of Medicine in Portland, Oregon, a residency in radiology at University of Colorado School of Medicine in Denver, Colorado, and a fellowship in nuclear medicine at Johns Hopkins University School of Medicine in Baltimore, Maryland.

At the end of his training he returned to University of Colorado School of Medicine as head of nuclear medicine for seven years. Then he joined Radiology Imaging Associates, a large academically oriented private practice radiology group in Denver. After twenty-five years in private practice he returned to University of Colorado School of Medicine, again as head of nuclear medicine.

www.ingramcontent.com/pod-product-compliance
Lightning Source LLC
Chambersburg PA
CBHW051513260626
47162CB00008B/2950